PRAISE FOR M. L. BUCHMAN

3x "Top 10 Romance of the Year"

— BOOKLIST

13 times "Top Pick of the Month"

— NIGHT OWL REVIEWS

I became completely immersed in this story and it had me at page one. Entertaining and full of emotion.

— FRESH FICTION, *WHERE DREAMS ARE BORN*

A delightful family drama with a feel good storyline. Readers will relish this entertaining contemporary.

— MIDWEST BOOK REVIEW, *WHERE DREAMS
UNFOLD*

A favorite author of mine. I'll read anything that carries his name, no questions asked. Meet your new favorite author!

— THE SASSY BOOKSTER, FLASH OF FIRE

M.L. Buchman is guaranteed to get me lost in a good story.

I love Buchman's writing. His vivid descriptions bring everything to life in an unforgettable way.

Buchman has catapulted his way to the top tier of my favorite authors.

The only thing you'll ask yourself is, "When does the next one come out?"

Superb! Miranda is utterly compelling!

Miranda Chase continues to astound and charm.

Escape Rating: A. Five Stars! OMG just start with *Drone* and be prepared for a fantastic binge-read!

# WHERE DREAMS CONTINUE

## A PIKE PLACE MARKET SEATTLE ROMANCE

## M. L. BUCHMAN

Buchman Bookworks

# Other works by M. L. Buchman:

## Contemporary Romance (cont)

Love Abroad
*Heart of the Cotswolds: England*
*Path of Love: Cinque Terre, Italy*

Where Dreams
*Where Dreams are Born*
*Where Dreams Reside*
*Where Dreams Are of Christmas\**
*Where Dreams Unfold*
*Where Dreams Are Written*
*Where Dreams Continue*

## Science Fiction / Fantasy

Deities Anonymous
*Cookbook from Hell: Reheated*
*Saviors 101*

Single Titles
*The Nara Reaction*
*Monk's Maze*
*the Me and Elsie Chronicles*

## Non-Fiction

Strategies for Success
*Managing Your Inner Artist/Writer*
*Estate Planning for Authors\**
*Character Voice*
*Narrate and Record Your Own*
*Audiobook\**

# Short Story Series by M. L. Buchman:

## Romantic Suspense

Antarctic Ice Fliers

Delta Force
*Th Delta Force Shooters*
*The Delta Force Warriors*

Firehawks
*The Firehawks Lookouts*
*The Firehawks Hotshots*
*The Firebirds*

The Night Stalkers
*The Night Stalkers 5D Stories*
*The Night Stalkers 5E Stories*
*The Night Stalkers CSAR*
*The Night Stalkers Wedding Stories*

US Coast Guard

White House Protection Force

## Contemporary Romance

Eagle Cove

Henderson's Ranch⁺

Where Dreams

## Action-Adventure Thrillers

Dead Chef

Miranda Chase Origin Stories

## Science Fiction / Fantasy

Deities Anonymous

Other
*The Future Night Stalkers*
*Single Titles*

# CONTENTS

# ABOUT THIS TITLE

Five stories about finding meaning and romance in Seattle's eclectic Pike Place Market.

- *Where Dreams Taste Like Chocolate* – When a chocolatier gets a taste for a fashion powerhouse, can he capture her dreams in a simple confection?
- *Where Dreams Are Sewn* – She has always sewn dreams for others but now she must stitch together her own future if she dares.
- *Where Dreams Are Well Done* – When cooking in the country's top Italian restaurant is no longer enough, can he shape a dish to win her love?
- *Where Dreams Thrive* – She found a new mother in *Where Dreams Unfold.* Now grown, can she find a dream of her own?
- *Where Dreams Begin* – Years ago, three college girls came to Seattle for Christmas. Little did they know that it would change their lives forever and set them all on the path where dreams come true.

# WHERE DREAMS TASTE LIKE CHOCOLATE

**Tony Bosco,** *itinerant chocolatier, returned to Seattle to work in his cousin's shop; a legacy from their past. But only when he searches for the heart behind their granddad's recipes does he begin to discover his own gifts.*

**Raquel Wells** *has been instrumental in creating the business success of Perrin's Glorious Garb clothiers. Her weekly treat, two pieces of Bosco chocolate. Next? Find the man to fulfill Stage Three of her Personal Life Plan, which is right on track, until her meticulous agenda is sideswiped by Tony.*

*Their futures await Where Dreams Taste Like Chocolate.*

# CHAPTER 1

"*Madonna Mother of God!*" It was a good thing that Grandma wasn't here or she'd have smacked her wooden spoon on the crown of his head, but Tony Bosco couldn't help himself.

His cousin Vic looked up from where he'd been sliding the latest tray of dark chocolate orange truffles into the display case. Together they stared out the large plate-glass window that faced onto the Madison Street sidewalk, at the east edge of Seattle.

"Oh, yes. She is something, isn't she?"

*Something?* Tony couldn't even speak. He hadn't prayed in years but he wanted to drop to his knees on the linoleum and beg God himself to make her turn in at their chocolate shop's door. He'd been back in Seattle for only three hours and he had just seen a goddess—unlike any woman he'd found in his entire five years in Europe.

When she did indeed turn toward him, he considered maybe Grandma was right and he should start going back to church.

With a bright tinkle of the bells on the back of the door, she breezed in. Five-ten of statuesque redhead in a flirty dress—the shade of beaten copper that clung to her like a dusting of sugar —strolled into the shop. The calf-high boots and accompanying short hem on the dress didn't *imply* a thing; it shouted "Amazing woman!"

"I need two of your finest, Vic. It's a beautiful Friday."

Tony couldn't have said it better himself.

Vic already had a pair of his ginger caramel dark chocolates in a tiny sack. He exchanged them for the six dollars she already had out in her hand, her long graceful hand.

With a cheery, *"Ciao!"* she was gone out the door and Tony was left listening to the ringing bell rather than that silky voice, American English, but seasoned with Italian. Gone so fast he didn't even have an eye color for her, though an impression of bright blue existed somewhere in his head.

"What the hell was that?" He still didn't have his breath back.

Vic laughed, "Don't worry. You'll never get used to her. But every Friday, if she's had a good week, she comes and buys two dark chocolate ginger caramels. Won't buy anything else, so I make sure to never run out on a Friday."

"And if she's had a bad week?"

"Don't see her, but thankfully that doesn't happen so much. I do so look forward to Fridays."

"Couldn't you have, like, slowed her down for a moment?" Tony knew he hadn't blinked, and still there hadn't been a chance to look at her clearly. Too many first impressions and too little time to sort through them. He sniffed the air, but could find not one hint of her. Only the rich smell of fine chocolate remained in the shop.

"Can't be done."

"Because you haven't tried."

"Tried plenty, Cuz. Not happening."

Tony rolled his eyes at his cousin. Vic had always been a lame-ass when it came to meeting girls. Actually, he'd been stellar at it, as long as Tony wasn't around. Tony always managed first choice, which he only lorded over his cousin at every *other* opportunity, not wanting to be too obnoxious.

Vic laughed at him, "Okay, Mr. Hotshot European Chocolatier. Next week, I'll keep my big mouth shut, you go ahead and try. Not a thing on this planet is gonna slow that woman down."

He didn't want her to slow down, he certainly never did that himself. He just wanted to move down the same path for a length or two, long enough for a wild affair. Tony turned back to the chocolate-making work counter and looked down at what Vic had given him on his return to the States just hours before.

His cousin had taken over the shop and the family recipes when their shared grandparents had retired and gone RVing. He'd never thought they were the sort, impossible to imagine them *not* in this shop. But they were off to tour every scenic byway in the country.

He'd never really thought he'd be back here. He'd worked in some of Europe's premier chocolateries and been trained by master chefs, but the old shop felt comfortable. It was the right size. A cozy front area for customers to stare into the large glass display cases, small enough for a friendly jostling of elbows as they picked and chose, but not cramped or crowded. The kitchen was behind, with no door to hide it away from the curious who wanted to peek over the cabinets. Light streamed in, bright through the front glass, dappled by trees through the high, kitchen windows in back.

This shop is where the two boys had spent every summer as kids. Once Vic had taken over, he'd increased business to the point where he could either manage the shop or make the chocolates, but not both. Seattle loved chocolate treats, and had plenty of companies catering to that craving. But even with competition, Granddad's recipes were making a name for The Chocolaterie Bosco.

Tony had been at his usual loose ends when Vic called. He'd

been hanging in Milan where his latest girlfriend had dumped him. Normally it worked the other way, but when the captain of the winning Italian team of the Tour de France swept her up, he knew he'd been totally outclassed. They'd been close to done anyway.

Il Cioccolato Bello only needed him for pick up work. He'd learned all he was going to at Oui Chocolat in Chartres outside of Paris. He'd plumbed the depths of Die Schokolade Maestro in Hamburg. And even thinking of the head chocolatiers at Kāko in New Zealand or Callebaut in Belgium made him exhausted, he was so not excited about "going back to school" yet again.

So, Vic had given him an excuse to move once more half around the world and come make chocolate for a small but enthusiastic clientele. Just the two of them and a part-time clerk on the weekend, closed Mondays and Tuesdays.

He leaned on the work counter and stared down at the dozens of hand-scribed index cards laid out across the cool marble slab. Vic had set them out for him. Granddad's sloppy handwriting was faded on some to near illegibility, partially lost behind chocolate smears on others, but there was a voice here. A voice Tony had seen and loved, but perhaps never really heard.

He picked up one that he thought might entice *la belle signora.*

"I'll start here," he held up the card.

"Courvoisier-brandied cherry," Vic nodded his approval. They shared a smile. They both remembered the trouble they'd earned for dropping a pair of them down the back of Vic's older sister's dress one summer then smacking them so that they burst, just moments before her date arrived. The long red stains had never come out and they'd both learned an appreciation— over many, many tedious unpaid hours of manual labor at the shop—just how much fine girl clothes cost.

# CHAPTER 2

*Raquel Wells sat in* Madison Park, counting an extra
blessing that her favorite bench was open. It sat at
the edge of the park, under the shade of a tall maple tree and
faced Lake Washington. As she opened the paper bag she looked
out at the lake: twenty miles long and three wide, it had halted
the eastward expansion of Seattle a century before. Most of the
park was fronted by a sandy beach and a very popular swimming area. Her favorite stretch was perched above a rocky rip-
rap and nestled under friendly maple trees close by the shore.

From here, downtown Seattle was a comforting four miles
behind her and the broad lake masked any thoughts of Bellevue
on the far shore. Here is where she did her best thinking. Here
is where she ate the best chocolate she'd ever found.

Vic Bosco's Ginger Caramel, the dark chocolate sheen ever
so lightly dusted with sea salt, slayed her every time. This is
what heaven was like: a sunny day, a beautiful view, and a multi-
layered treat for her palate.

As an extra treat today, her outfit had totally gobsmacked
Vic's new assistant. The guy looked as if he'd been paralyzed.
Having an outfit that actually made a man's jaw drop, well, that

was a definite bonus. He was six foot of terribly handsome and appeared to be one of those guys completely willing to wield it as a woman-slayer. Absolutely not her type.

Her dress was just one of the many benefits of working at Perrin's Glorious Garb. Four years ago she'd taken over as store manager on a wing, a prayer, and at the sharp prodding of two of Perrin's best friends. Perrin had been barely scraping by and Raquel had been doing no better as an underling in the corporate mayhem of Seattle. Perrin had offered her straight commission and a ten percent share in the company if it survived.

Many times it had been close, but Perrin's talent couldn't be stopped. Now, with Perrin's recent successes and Melanie Harper signing aboard as CEO, the company had gained global attention.

Raquel had kept the operation going, taken night classes for an MBA (Stage One of her Personal Life Plan), and scrabbled like a madwoman for four years.

And at a very fine luncheon this afternoon, Perrin and Melanie had presented her with a brand new business card; it read "CFO"—Chief Financial Officer. There had been champagne, there had been tears, and there had been many smiles of well-deserved satisfaction. Soon, if the five-year business plan that she herself had written came even close to being accurate, they were all going to be very wealthy women.

That was completely worthy of two of Vic Bosco's ginger caramels.

She'd promoted her clerk to store manager and was now free to focus on the on-line retail side of the business. Part of it was straightforward; Perrin's unusual designs built to stock. But Perrin's trademark was custom clothing matched to the individual. Turning that into an electronic platform was proving to be a fun challenge and a potentially lucrative one.

It was all running smoothly, or as smoothly as such things did. A lot of hard work lay ahead for all of them. But thankfully it was no longer about survival, rather it was about creating a stable success. That was Stage Two.

So, now it was time to focus on the next Stage Three of her Personal Life Plan: find a suitable partner. That too promised to be a great deal of fun and, if all went well, that too would have life-changing results.

She bit into sweet, salt, and ginger and let her eyes drift shut to fully appreciate the chocolate flavors.

## CHAPTER 3

*he very first thing* that Tony changed was how Vic was making the chocolate itself.

"Only the Criollo beans, buddy. Forastero is for wimps and Trinitario is only for wannabes and second raters."

"But—"

"Deal with it. Sell your stock off to some other shop. I won't be using it."

They had always mixed and ground their own nibs. The process of separating the cocoa solids and the cocoa butter was slow but worth the quality control it provided. Then they remixed them in precise portions with sugar, milk for the milk chocolate, and sometimes other flavorings. Granddad had always taught them to conch the chocolate for a full twenty-four hours. Chocolate was tenaciously gritty until it was ground with metal beads to break it down. Tony jumped the twenty-four hours to three full days—for mouthfeel, a trade secret he'd learned while sleeping with a pretty little Swedish chocolatier named Rosalie.

He forced Vic to buy a second conching machine so that they could run dark and milk chocolate batches at the same time. Vic went totally lame and bought a small machine without consulting him.

Tony dug into his savings and bought a large capacity machine for the dark chocolate. He'd never been a fan of white chocolate, so the small machine that Vic had bought got demoted to that role. Granddad's old homebuilt could run the milk chocolate.

"It's Friday, buddy. You ready, *mi cugino?*" Vic elbowed him sharply enough in the ribs to knock the air out of him.

"Not an idiot, my cousin," Tony waited until Vic's guard was down and slipped an ice cube down the back of his shirt. He'd been thinking about the Madonna Lady all week. How was it that his idiot cousin hadn't even learned her name.

It was a beautiful June day. What would she be wearing on this bright, breezy day by the lake?

The answer once again took his breath away. Parisians so proud of their fashion sense didn't have an inch of advantage on this woman. She breezed into the shop. A diaphanous lavender skirt that swirled about her knees and a matching leather vest, one of the sleeveless ones never intended to close, simply to enhance—a duty it performed admirably well because after all, it had a lot to work with. The luminous blue of her blouse matched her sapphire eyes.

She was looking at him with a single arched eyebrow, six dollars already in her fine-fingered hands.

*Speak!* Tony shouted at himself. "Greetings, Madonna Lady. How may I help you?"

"She—"

Tony cut Vic off with a scathing look. He knew what she wanted, that wasn't the point. The point was to get her talking.

Vic winced. His cousin knew he'd botched the play.

Raquel was smiling at him. Okay, he'd have to kill Vic later for making him look a fool, even if it had been his own fault.

"Two of your dark chocolate ginger caramels."

He offered her a small sample plate of chocolates, "Would you like to try my granddad's brandied cherries?"

"No thank you. Just my two dark caramels."

In moments the door was closing with its cheery bell and six dollars rested beside the register.

"Gone..." he couldn't believe that she'd slipped away so easily. Not correcting his "Madonna Lady." Not offering her name in its stead. And turning down the chocolate he'd made especially for her, as good a treat as Granddad had ever concocted.

"Told ya. No slowing her down." Vic slapped him on the back hard enough to really sting and turned to greet a mother-daughter pair who entered the shop.

Her departing wave had been offhand, too perfectly casual. Tony knew when the gauntlet had been thrown down and he wasn't a man to leave that challenge unanswered.

# CHAPTER 4

*R*aquel *sat on her* park bench and bit into the caramel. The chocolate slid over her tongue. It didn't simply melt in her mouth as usual. Instead, it hesitated to play there a while, thick with teasing flavors she'd never noticed before. She tilted her head to one side, watching a sailboat skim along the lake while appreciating. The cocoa taste built and lasted, like a sweet, pure chord from a harp.

Perhaps she was extra sensitive today because she was launching Stage Three of her Personal Life Plan tonight. In two hours she'd be having dinner with Steven Tu. He was one of the partners of the law firm that Perrin used when her friend Jo was too busy. He was hugely successful and quite handsome. They'd met at business functions a few times. His sense of humor was a little weak, but his intelligence and taste more than compensated.

Raquel had always worked hard, unlike either of her parents. They came from money and were well on their way to losing it all through benign neglect. She was going the opposite direction and had been since she was seven. Her net worth had always been known to the penny and ruthlessly budgeted. She had started with hand sewing doll dresses for sale at Saturday markets; even working by flashlight under the covers until her fingers were poked to bleeding. Making clothes for junior high and high school friends, at least the ones who cared more about looks than designer labels, had given her a good training. She'd also learned that while she'd never be a designer, she could copy a name brand and knew how to reshape it to a body. She'd put herself through college working three jobs and still had been doing that when she'd joined Perrin's shop.

Now after two decades, she was twenty-seven and all of that work was paying off. Raquel Wells was about to collect her rewards. Not that achieving her goals had ever slowed her down; she'd just set new ones and continue charging upward. Financially stable at twenty-seven. Next on the list was happily married by thirty. She'd allotted three years to make sure it was the right man for her, though she only expected to use six months of that time. True financial success and solid personal stability by thirty-two, plenty of time for a child at thirty-five.

When Raquel began considering which man she might choose to build that future with, Steven Tu's gentle manners and impeccable taste came easily to mind.

She had come up with a list of three initial candidates and hoped that one of them would be the answer she was looking for.

Another rustle of the bag, and the second caramel was gone before she managed to slow herself down enough to assess what was actually occurring.

The chocolate was different.

She didn't like that. Vic Bosco's chocolate was comfortable, familiar, it fit into her life. For the last year, since she first felt she could afford the splurge, it had been both exceptional and completely consistent. You could plan on exactly what you were going to get there.

This must be the doing of the one playing games at the counter, the one fishing for her name with "Madonna Lady."

She should go back and tell Vic to change it back, or get rid of the new man. But then Raquel realized that she was still tasting other aspects of the chocolate, though the treat was long gone. The flavors were different, but they were also lusher and richer. They continued to open and unfold despite how greedily she'd eaten both candies.

Maybe she wouldn't be complaining to Vic. Somehow it felt disloyal to Vic to even think that. But it was...better.

Rising from her bench, she smoothed the chocolatier's bag, folded it in half, and slipped it into her skirt pocket. Time to go change for Steven.

# CHAPTER 5

*T*ony *was losing his* mind.

Three more weeks. No joy.

She'd refused a Habañero Mango Crème. She'd scoffed at his Pear Brandy Truffle. And now she'd even turned down his taste of Christmas in Summertime Strawberry Eggnog with just a hint of nutmeg.

He'd tried slipping the treat into the bag with her invariant ginger caramels, but she'd caught him the first time.

The second time, he had placed it into the bag *before* she came in. She had actually brought that bag back after she was done eating her two caramels.

Placing the bag on the top of the glass display case, she'd simply said, "I didn't pay for this." And then shot him a wicked smile. With a swirl of red hair and a jingle of the door's bell, she was back out of the store. The shop was far too busy with a Seattle Chocolate Tour for him to respond. Vic had one thing right, the woman apparently never slowed down.

After that last failure to entice her, he didn't even try to put a third candy in the bag.

Today the Madonna Lady didn't even open it to check.

Instead she raised the bag a few times as if weighing it, smiled at him, then paid and departed. He'd been left to watch the effect of designer slacks on mile-long legs and a well-toned behind. A fine view, but not what he was really hankering for.

Clearly she had a plan: to make him totally insane.

Just as clearly, he needed a plan. The problem with a plan was that it required thinking ahead. Even without his cousin's constant ribbing, he knew that wasn't his strongest suit. Vic had always been the thinker and Tony had always gone with the flow. He was only ever serious about one thing: chocolate.

Like it was yesterday, he still remembered the first time that he'd watched, really watched, his grandfather forming a chilled ganache into a perfect ball, swirling it in melted chocolate to coat it, then giving it a quick roll in cocoa powder and coconut. Granddad had popped it into Tony's mouth, still cold in the center, the chocolate coating still warm beneath the cocoa and coconut. In that moment he knew what he wanted to do. He wanted to awe someone the way Granddad had awed him that long-ago day.

And there was the problem.

The beautiful redhead wasn't even giving him a chance to impress her. So why was this one woman so important that she was making him doubt his skills as a chocolatier?

*Answer that one, boy, and you could conquer the world.* Grand-dad's standard reply to so many of Tony's questions wasn't comforting, but at least it was familiar.

"Vic, I gotta go for a swim."

"Yeah, you look like you need to soak your head."

Tony punched Vic's upper arm hard, with a knuckle extended to ping the nerve cluster, and then headed to the apartment they shared above the shop to change.

# CHAPTER 6

"*O*h my God!"

Raquel looked up from her second caramel to see Vic's assistant halted in mid-stride mere steps from her bench. She had to blink. Not wearing a chef's coat and slacks, he was almost unrecognizable. He wore an old pair of cut-off shorts that revealed powerful legs, a t-shirt that clung to his frame, and a towel around his neck. He was a very handsome man in his chef's suit. But out of it? Wow!

She primarily sold women's clothes, but Perrin occasionally did menswear and Raquel knew enough about the male physique to see that he had a swimmer's build. Not as a mere occasional workout; he obviously swam a lot to earn such conditioning.

"Madonna Lady," he breathed it out on a gasp of disbelief.

"That's not my name."

"So, what *is* your name?" he growled in frustration.

"Raquel Wells. And if you make one single joke about Raquel Welch and fur bikinis, you're a dead man." She'd heard that way too many times. That was one of the reasons she liked Steven Tu, he hadn't gone there once in their month of dating, without prompting. The man presently standing by "her" bench she knew she had to warn off, a fact confirmed by his smile though he asked a different question.

"Why didn't you tell my your name before?"

"You didn't ask."

He stared down at his flip-flops and then up at the leaves of the overhanging maple tree before shaking his head sadly and laughing.

"You're right, I didn't."

And as simple as that Steven Tu was crossed off her list. This hadn't been much of a joke, but the man had laughed at it none-theless. Steven had not even less of a sense of humor than she'd first thought. They'd been compatible enough on other fronts—both business people, both very forthright—for it to be a possibility. But the chocolatier's simple laugh had disproven that it was enough.

"May I join you?" he waved to the empty end of the bench.

Manners were appreciated, even from a man she could never be interested in, so she nodded her assent. "And what is your name?"

"Oh, I'm not nearly so easy."

"I could ask Vic." She wasn't easy either, but she wasn't above being sneaky.

"You could. My cousin is a complete and total pushover around beautiful women."

"Whereas you are…"

"…much further into the complete idiot category. You can call me Tony."

"But that's not your name?"

His shrug was eloquent.

Now it was her turn to laugh. There was a scream of five-year old giggles that rippled over from the nearby beach. She took the last bite of the caramel that had been melting in her fingers. "That's so good. How do you do that?" She licked her fingers clean.

"Family secret. I could tell you, but then…" he shrugged negligently.

"You'd have to kill me."

He nodded, "Sadly true. That or marry you. Then you'd be family. What do you say, is that secret worth being married to me for ever and ever?"

Not a chance. "Maybe I'll marry Victor instead. That way I'd be family and you'd have to tell me." Tony didn't look even a little like a for ever-and-ever sort of guy.

"It's Vicenzo. And if you marry Vic, then I'd definitely have to kill him," again the deep snarl sounded though it was belied by an easy smile. "I know fratricide is frowned upon, but you can't really get in trouble for killing a first cousin, can you? I mean if he goes off and marries the most beautiful woman I've ever seen, he deserves what he gets."

"He does." She felt another laugh bubbling up inside her. He was quick, this chocolatier perhaps named Tony. And charming. Raquel generally enjoyed her power over men. But she was looking for someone who: 1) saw past her beauty and, 2) had more to offer than charm. She'd estimate a poor rate of return on a bet that Tony could manage either one.

She rose lightly to her feet, "I really must go. I have a date."

"A date?" Tony slapped a hand to his chest, slouched in the bench and groaned. "Is it serious? Can you be cured?"

"Yes. No. And yes." She was actually going to go and break her date with Steven, no point in wasting more time there when she knew it wasn't going to work out in the long term.

Tony started to look hopeful, but kept his hand on his heart as if in precaution.

"But not for you, my bucko."

He collapsed onto the bench as if dead and she laughed.

Then she turned for home. With Steven crossed off her list,

it was time to call Gary Thomas. Perrin's husband worked at Emerald City Opera and had introduced her to the new head of accounting there. A single father with a cute five-year-old girl. She'd met them both at Opera events and they were so charming together. In addition to their shared business backgrounds, Gary was clearly a sweet man with a big heart. Instant family could be both efficient and lovingly secure.

# CHAPTER 7

*J*t *was while he* was getting in an hour's swim on Lake Washington, the bracing water knocking some sense into him, that Tony figured out that he'd literally stumbled onto his plan. The next Friday he was ready.

Raquel breezed into the shop with her six dollars and ever-present smile. He took her money, handed over her pre-filled bag, then lifted one of his own and sent her a questioning glance.

Her smile quirked up on one side and lit her eyes. Damn! And he'd thought she was a knock-out before. That's when he understood that a regular smile was her default state. But it was only when it went sideways that he'd really tickled her funny bone.

She tipped her head to the side, causing her hair to cascade down over one shoulder in thick waves that just begged to be gently brushed back from her face. Then with a nod, she turned for the door.

Tony held up a hand palm out toward his cousin.

Vic automatically raised his hand, not really sure why. Tony slapped it with a hard high-five. This time it was Vic's jaw that was down.

Tony shed his jacket, grabbed his bag of chocolates, and bolted for the door so as not to lose Raquel. She didn't slow down a moment and he had to jog to catch up with those long legs.

Her bench was taken so they strolled along the pathways of Madison Park, past playgrounds loud with pre-dinnertime mobs of kids, along the winding walkway above the equally popular beach, and under the small section of quieter trees. It wasn't a big park, so the view was constantly changing: the cluster of shops at the end of Madison Street, a beach full of kids, a pretty little garden of rose bushes, shade trees, and from everywhere the sun sparkling off the surface of the lake.

As they walked, they talked of what she did for a living. At first he thought she just sold clothes, but as CFO of a rising clothier she was way more. A bit daunting, in fact, because even he'd heard of Perrin's Glorious Garb. The only thing about clothes that he usually paid attention to was how to take them off a willing woman. But Raquel was part of a powerhouse company that had commanded the cover and a major spread in the latest *SI* swimsuit issue. The fabulous Melanie claiming her fifth cover.

He, on the other hand, was an assistant in his cousin's chocolate shop. His only stake in the business was a shared heritage and a conching machine. It rapidly became clear that she was a very focused gal. She clearly ate, slept, and breathed the fashion business. He just didn't rate.

But as they strolled by the water and talked, he began to feel less overwhelmed. She wasn't some accounting nerd; she was as passionate for the business of clothing as he was for chocolate. It appeared to rise from that same deep core, reaching back into childhood and superseding all else.

*That* was a passion he could appreciate.

As summer drifted toward fall, they continued to walk or sit together on the bench each Friday. He'd never spent so much time with a woman he wasn't sleeping with, but it was hard to complain as he was so enjoying their weekly afternoons together.

She still refused to taste his chocolates, though he brought a different one each week. It had become a thing between them: he would plumb the depths of another of Granddad's recipes, and she would politely insist that she was happy with ones she knew.

# CHAPTER 8

*R*aquel *finally gave in* and tasted the chocolate from Tony's bag after an entire summer of Fridays. Their maple tree was starting to change colors, and maybe that too was part of the reason she gave in. She hadn't refused because she was stuck in her ways, as he'd jokingly accused her. Nor that she was a one-track gal, which she was, but not about chocolate. It was that she'd found what she wanted and that's what she ordered each week.

But mostly, he'd finally looked so pitiful that she'd broken down. How was she supposed to deny those sad, puppy dog eyes on six-one of pouting chocolatier male.

But this she hadn't expected. Liquid coconut trapped in a dark, dark chocolate.

"Oh my God!"

"Madonna Lady likes?" he'd insisted on continuing to call her that.

She could only close her eyes and nod. It didn't have the comfort of her ginger caramel, but it was so very good. It revealed exactly how skilled he was.

This chocolate didn't indicate a level of mere competence, it revealed mastery. The coconut didn't overwhelm, it whorled with and enhanced the perfectly smooth chocolate coating. All of his years studying in Europe had definitely not been as idle as he'd made them sound; this small confection could only be the result of years of remarkably focused training.

She sighed again as she finished the treat. This time it was a sad sigh, so she kept it to herself. She was jolted out of her small ennui by Tony.

"So, how's this next guy on your list working out?"

Gary Thomas was sweet, thoughtful, and a good businessman. After three months together, they'd even begun talking about when it might be time for her to meet his daughter as girlfriend rather than friend. They both agreed that it was too soon, but they were talking about it.

The problem with Gary was that he was merely a good businessman, not a *great* one, and definitely not a driven one. There was competence, but no passion. No mastery like Tony's chocolate nor the desire to achieve it.

Raquel had worked her fair share of nights and weekends, both while attending night school for her MBA and since for the growth of Perrin's Glorious Garb.

Gary had taken the job at Emerald City Opera as a downshift from a Microsoft job. His wife, a software engineer, hadn't wanted the downshift which had ultimately caused the breakdown of the marriage. The only time his ex took off work was to spend time with her daughter; something Raquel easily understood, but Gary didn't.

Raquel was a long way from ready to slow down. Along with Perrin's Glorious Garb, she was just picking up speed.

So. That left only one more man on her first-tier list. Marco Mancini was a division manager at Ferragamo Milan and he was all about speed.

"Milan?" Tony looked at her cross-eyed. "Why would you go to Milan for a date?"

She hadn't really meant to talk about her love life with the likes of Tony Bosco, but somehow it had become a natural part of their conversation.

For three months he'd listened and offered no comment, other than the one time clutching his heart. After she'd walked away from that first meeting at the bench, a final glance back had revealed him lying on the bench, hands crossed on his chest holding up his swimming towel as if it was a lily. She'd left him with her laughter.

Sometimes their Friday walks had become Friday meals; the edges of Madison Park boasted several nice restaurants. He never pushed any intimacy, said he never poached on another man's ground, he never even asked to come in when he walked her the few blocks to home on the warm evenings.

He kept it light. Sometimes he made her wonder if she was losing her powers, then she'd catch him watching her at unexpected moments. No, the interest continued, but the decency stopped him, as she was seeing another man. But now Marco Mancini was next on her Stage Three list.

She and Marco had met at New York Fashion Week last February. The heat between them had been instantaneous. Their affair had been wild, crammed in between runway shows and designer meetings. Their postcoital conversations had been purely business and marketing—which had been fun; sometimes even during sex—which had been perhaps a bit much. His focus was incredible and his skill as a lover was amazing. He had made it very clear in several very suggestive e-mails quite how happy he would be to see her again. She would suggest a week's visit to start, and see where that led them.

# CHAPTER 9

"*Milan?" Tony asked the* darkness above his bed.

"Milan?" he asked the bathroom mirror a couple of hours later, still unable to sleep.

He went back to bed...for seventeen minutes. It was the middle of the goddamn night, but his brain didn't seem to care.

"Milan?" he muttered to the chocolate conching machine grinding its way to a finish of the latest batch of dark chocolate.

He flipped through the battered wooden box of Granddad's recipes. He stopped at the one with a small heart drawn in the upper-right corner. It was the chocolate he'd made sixty years ago for the woman he'd been courting. So simple it was laughable, so pure that the least mistake would ruin it. Chocolate-covered blueberries. This one card was covered with a dozen tiny corrections. He'd clearly worked and reworked this recipe until he had it perfect.

But that was his grandfather and grandmother's story. He didn't want to give Raquel anything more of Granddad's, he wanted...

He didn't know what. He wasn't used to wanting more. Not when it came to women.

But he'd start by closing the age-worn wooden box.

The kitchen had filled with the fall morning's light by the time Vic wandered into the kitchen, "It's time to open up. What are you working on?"

Tony ignored him and threw his latest attempt into the trash.

At some point Vic set a sandwich and a soda beside his marble work table. Tony could hear the noise of customers out front, of the Saturday crowd as it swelled, then later faded away. The windows were dark by the time he finished his creation.

Vic sat quietly in a dark corner of the kitchen with a glass of red wine, waiting.

Tony set the finished chocolate on a cut-glass plate and delivered it to his cousin.

In silence, Vic took it, bit off a small corner and closed his eyes the way Granddad used to when analyzing a taste.

Vic took his time, finishing the piece in three small bites, taking a long time after each.

When he finished and reopened his eyes, Tony could feel the nerves coursing under his skin. He was never twitchy about making chocolate, but this one was different. This one was…

Vic rose to his feet without a word. He crossed to the office nook and returned. He set a blank index card and a pen on the table in front of Tony before returning to his seat.

"You have to write that one down. And, as Granddad always said, 'Don't give me any crap about it being in your head, boy.' It's better than anything Granddad ever did. He's going to freak out the next time he and Grandma come through town. Christ, Antonio, it's amazing."

Tony wrote it down, his hand shaking with lack of sleep.

CHAPTER 10

"*G*one? *What do you* mean gone?" Tony wanted to reach through the phone and strangle the pleasant woman on the far end of the line. He didn't have Raquel's number, so he'd called Perrin's Glorious Garb as soon as he'd woken up. The front desk clerk hadn't been at all helpful about her boss' private schedule, so he'd bucked his way up the food chain, never expecting to be handed right to the owner herself.

"She's on vacation," Perrin's voice was polite and distant. "How may I help you?"

"Between Friday night and Sunday morning? She can't be in Milan already." Tony closed his eyes, struggling not to imagine Raquel in the arms of some hot Italian designer. His stomach twisted.

"No, she's staying overnight with some friends in New York." The voice shifted as if he suddenly had the woman's full attention. "Is this the One?"

"The one what?"

The woman on the phone sounded even merrier at his confusion. "Well, you better do something quick, Mister One. Raquel doesn't slow down for any man."

Where had he heard that before.

"When are you expecting her back?"

"Wrong question. Lose one turn. Ehhh!" She made a harsh penalty-buzzer noise.

He pulled the phone away from his ear and stared at it for a moment. "Then what's the right question?"

"Ehhhhhhhh!" Perrin made a longer buzzer sound.

"Oh." His only excuse was that he'd slept under six of the last forty-eight hours. He knew the right question now.

"She's only staying in New York one night?"

"Give the man a kewpie doll!" It sounded oddly as if the woman on the other end of the phone was now dancing.

# CHAPTER 11

*I*t *was Monday afternoon* by the time Raquel came off the New York-Milan flight. She felt ragged. All of the expectation she'd thought to be feeling hadn't made the flight with her. Not even in her checked luggage. She'd slept poorly in New York and not at all on either flight. It wasn't supposed to be like this.

She must look awful. Marco was going to take one look at her after she came through customs and tell her to turn back around. Even her lack of enthusiasm had a lack of enthusiasm.

When Marco had said how excited he would be to see her any time, and Perrin had teased her about backlogged vacation time, she booked a flight and took a chance. She could keep up with the business on her tablet computer and enjoy Italy and Marco in between. Multi-tasking was her lifestyle.

Except it didn't feel that way.

At the head of the jetway she stumbled to a halt. A beautiful man in a white dress shirt, dark slacks, and mirrored sunglasses stood just inside the terminal. The sign said, "Wells."

Marco had said he'd meet her at the hotel. But he'd sent

someone? No one should be waiting for her on this side of customs and security anyway.

Then she focused her tired eyes on the rest of the card, "Fur bikinis for sale—cheap."

She laughed. Someone had—

Finally she looked up at his face.

"Tony?"

"Antonio Alberico Bosco at your service. That's my full name, which oddly means 'invaluable elf ruler of the woods' if you can believe that."

He had her laughing despite her confusion and exhaustion. She couldn't make sense of it; of any of it.

"My flight made it in fourteen hours ahead of yours. I slept over there," he pointed at a row of seats close to the gate. With an easy confidence, he took her arm and led her to that quiet corner of the terminal's seating. The vast windows revealed the paved expanse of the airport and the city skyscrapers rising beyond.

"I'm..." she took a deep breath to steady her whirling mind, "...meeting someone."

"Yes, me."

"But—"

"Open wide."

"What?"

"Open wide or you won't get your treat."

She looked down. He held a small box marked with The Chocolaterie Bosco logo, gold on black. It had always looked abstract...but she now saw that it was an elf playing a trumpet beneath a tree—Antonio Alberico Bosco.

"You flew all this way to feed me a piece of chocolate?"

His engaging smile had her opening her mouth against her better judgment. How ludicrous was it? She was here for a tryst with a highly successful Italian designer and now she was sitting and tasting—

Her brain switched off as she bit down on the chocolate that Tony had slipped into her mouth. The chocolate was, oh, magnificent. Impossibly smooth and luscious. There was a hint of...it took her a moment to pin it down, fresh apricot.

Then her teeth broke into the center releasing a flood of apricot liqueur, thickened into a syrup that lit up her sense of taste and smell too, and then she finally sunk her teeth into perfect texture of the candied apricot core. Triple apricot!

Somehow, impossibly, Tony had captured their summer's worth of Fridays in a single bite: from the first change of the chocolate, to the lush mastery of the liquid coconut but transformed from tropical to summer, and the candied core texture that she so loved in the ginger caramel.

"It's like a perfect kiss," she barely managed to breath it out. She opened her eyes. Tony's handsome face so close that she'd barely have to move to touch noses.

Then Tony's lips brushed hers. It was a question, no more.

When she answered, he opened to her and slid his hand to cradle her cheek.

The kiss coursed through her. Men mostly just wanted to sleep with her, but against all odds, Tony had first become her friend. She knew how impressed he was by what she'd done, how deeply he understood the drive that had pushed them both every day, even if it had been down such different paths.

And his kiss, oh gods she was lost. His power overwhelmed her senses until she had to push him away so that she could breathe and think and hear something other than the pounding of her heart.

"How?" How had he known to be here? The passing crowd from her flight had thinned.

"Up 'til now I have always made Granddad's chocolates. Enhanced them. Built on them."

He disoriented her; he was answering a different question. He did that to her a lot. Tony Bosco the European playboy had also been the chocolate maestro. She'd watched through the summer as Chocolaterie Bosco had bloomed with him as the new chocolatier.

"I never understood how Granddad made such chocolate until I really looked at the recipe he'd used to court Grandma. He put his heart on the plate. You've done something to me, Raquel, and this is the best way I know how to show it."

She made herself focus on his words and resist her desire to kiss him again. His kiss was even better than his chocolate which should be impossible, but it was true.

"Since the first moment you swooped into the shop, there has only been one woman in my thought—" Then he burst out laughing. Not at something amusing, but at something impossibly funny.

For once she couldn't follow the joke, "What?" By the time he recovered enough to speak, she was ready to offer him a sharp jab.

"Your boss is a very smart woman."

Perrin was, but what did she have to do with apricot chocolate and the best kiss of her life?

"She said I was 'The One.' I had no idea what she was talking about, but I get it now."

Rachel tried to come up with an answer, but couldn't find it anywhere. "Okay, I give. You need to let me in on the joke."

His face sobered, then he brushed his fingers along her cheek. "I'm, uh, glad you liked the chocolate."

"It was magnificent, but that was also a subject change."

"It was," he nodded. "For perhaps the first time, I wasn't copying Granddad."

"You put your heart on the plate."

He managed a nod, but his lips were clamped tight as if he was unwilling to speak the next words.

He really had put his heart into it. No one else could have

made that, could have captured their story in a confection. What had it cost him to do it? And he'd done it for her. He'd—

"You just told me how you made that incredible bite."

"I did," his voice was rough.

"So, having revealed your secret, now you have to kill me?"

He shook his head.

"Well, I'm certainly not going to marry your cousin in exchange for that secret."

All of his suppressed tension exploded outward in a laugh that had heads turning in their direction.

"Thank God for that." Then he slipped out of the chair beside her and knelt on the floor of the airport terminal without releasing her hands. "Will you marry me for it, Raquel? For I can't imagine ever designing a chocolate for anyone else but you."

In Raquel's neatly ordered life, it made absolutely no sense. Yet it made perfect sense. They shared passion and determination and he had a heart that she knew would never stop giving. He'd opened up a place in her that she didn't even know existed and filled it with light and smiles and flavors. It was so easy to picture a life with him, children with him, growing old with him.

"I guess that depends."

He blinked at her in surprise.

"It depends on whether you were smart enough to bring more of that apricot chocolate."

"I did. And I'll make you as much as you ever want once we're home."

She leaned down to seal the deal with a kiss.

"Then let's go home."

# WHERE DREAMS ARE SEWN

*Lost dreams and shattered ones can be stitched back together.*

*__Kari Jones'__ dreams of becoming the next great fashion designer elude her. Lead fabricator for the next great designer works for her, mostly. But when asked to collaborate on a new teen line, Kari's dreams start coming true.*

*__Richard Nyberg's__ knowledge of women's fashion is limited to lighting them on the opera stage. Since his wife left, he struggles to raise his daughter himself. When she becomes a model for a new teen line, he encounters far more than he bargained for.*

*Their tattered dreams can only be reborn Where Dreams Are Sewn.*

# CHAPTER 1

"*You've got to be* kidding me."

"The woman is a demon," Clem agreed with her. Anna, Kristin, and Mitchell leaned in to look over their shoulders.

Kari Jones flipped up the hem of the dress to inspect the lie of the fabric. "Look at this seam work."

"Beyond demon," Anna agreed over Mitchell's low groan.

"Am not a demon!" Perrin stood at the entry to the sewing room. Her designs were always immaculate and technically a challenge, but this one took it to a whole new level.

"Then what are you?" Kari wanted to grow up to be like Perrin. Too bad it was never going to happen. That Kari was three days older than her boss was the least of the problems. She had learned the skills and could pattern and sew as well as her boss, perhaps even better, but the talent and vision that had struck down like a lightning bolt and launched Perrin into the fashion design firmament had somehow bypassed Kari.

Her own designs looked…serviceable.

Perrin's designs had walked runways and were splashed across major magazines.

When she took the job almost a year ago, Kari had hoped that some "designer magic" might rub off Perrin and onto her, but it hadn't happened so far. However, the amount she'd learned about construction was huge.

"How did you even do this?" Clem was still inspecting the dress. Kari could see the secrets and looked to be the only one of the five sewers who had.

"I'm a *demoness!*" Perrin did a football end-zone style dance around the dress form.

Kari snorted, "That's for damn sure. A very pregnant one."

Perrin rubbed her belly and smiled. She wasn't due for another couple months, but the blonde was already spectacularly round-bellied rather than her normal waif-slender self. Another reason Kari would never grow up to be Perrin; at six-foot Kari was two inches taller and far more curved—well, than Perrin's normal shape. Her non-descript dark hair curled to her shoulders instead of being a golden bob.

Still, she wished she could grow up to be Perrin someday.

Perrin continued a cha-cha toward the doorway of the room where the five sewers worked to reproduce Perrin's designs in necessary sizes for the shop and custom orders. The others continued deconstructing the new dress, learning from Perrin's prototype. Anna was a wizard with pattern-making and Clem was almost as good a seamstress as Kari was. They'd figure it out. Kristin and Mitchell were so fast that, once a design was understood, they could reproduce it as many times as necessary.

Perrin tipped her head for Kari to join her in the main design studio.

Kari hurried through the doorway, she loved this space. Folded fabrics shimmered along three walls, peeking out of floor-to-ceiling cubby holes abundant with color and texture. To the right another door led into the storefront and to the left a bank of high windows above the fabrics let in the Seattle sunshine, which today was of the typically autumn gray-and-wet variety. Down the center was a sprawling cutting table and another pair of sewing machines below the windows. Design heaven.

Tamara, Perrin's step-daughter, sat at the cutting table amidst a sea of fabrics. Even though they weren't related by blood, it was easy to see that the bolt of brilliance had landed on the fifteen-year-old's head as well. Tammy was piecing together a teen clothing line and it was some of the coolest work Kari had ever seen. With Tammy's work, she didn't feel envy; she felt awe.

Perrin perched carefully on a stool and Kari sat down facing her. Tammy looked up at her for a moment from across the table, but then returned her attention to the fabrics as if embarrassed; not even looking up long enough to offer a hello. Tammy Cullen was usually as effusive as her adoptive mother. And Kari had thought she was really close with the girl...but not at the moment.

Kari's nerves suddenly roared awake.

She turned her attention to Perrin and saw the worry there.

Kari couldn't imagine that she was about to be fired. Perrin's Glorious Garb needed to be adding more people, not cutting them. And she'd finally come to terms with not being Perrin...mostly.

But Perrin's worried look didn't go away. Not a good thing; she and Perrin tended to buoy each other up. The CEO could always calm them down, but Melanie was in Paris on her honeymoon.

"I—" they both started on the same breath.

Kari nodded for Perrin to speak first, and then had to wait her out.

"I," Perrin finally began again, "need you to do me a favor."

"Sure," Kari said in her most even voice. It didn't sound like she was being fired.

"Tammy's getting overwhelmed. Would you be willing to

take over as the head fabricator for her line?" Perrin spoke in a mad rush. "I know she's just fifteen and you'd rather be a designer but I want her to have the best and she's good on a machine but you're way better and you can do fitting even better than I can and I can't think of anyone that would be more fantastic or that we'd both trust more and—"

"Oh God, yes!" Kari managed to cut in on the runaway freight train of Perrin's words. Fifty percent relief and a hundred percent excitement.

"—because it's my daughter's line and I want it to be perfect and you could do that and…really?"

Kari nodded. Head seamstress on a new line? Oh yeah. And if it came out of Perrin's Glorious Garb, there was no question any line would be major; especially when it was as good as Tammy's. She'd been dying to get her hands on those designs.

"I was afraid you were about to fire me."

Perrin's shock shifted quickly to mock anger, "You try to leave here and you and I are going to have some harsh words. You belong here."

Kari could only smile back at her. She did. It was hard to believe, but Kari knew that she'd found exactly where she was supposed to be. It gave her a bit of a thrill that a woman of Perrin's amazing skills agreed.

"Really?" Tamara whispered from across the table, looking up shyly beneath the dark brows and hair she'd inherited from her birth mother who had passed on several years ago.

Kari rose and circled the table to sit beside Tamara. They were the ones who looked like mother and daughter. Everyone remarked on it who saw them together. It had become a running joke between them by the second time they'd met. They'd rapidly settled on Auntie and Little Girl.

"Are you kidding me? Your clothes rock. I'd love to help with them." Instead of offering the hug they normally shared, she held out a hand. "Thanks for asking for me."

They shook on it like two serious adults.

Then Tammy gave out a very fifteen-year-old squeal and threw herself into Kari's arms. "Love you, Auntie Kari."

Kari hugged her tight. This is what she wanted. Not just the challenge of helping shape a whole line. She buried her face in Tamara's hair for just a moment and wished she had a girl of her own.

"Love you...Big Girl."

Tammy squeezed her even tighter and squealed again, placing Kari's eardrum at serious risk.

# CHAPTER 2

*The moment he walked* in the shop, Richard Nyberg knew he'd made a mistake. *Always have an emergency book with you.* His wife had told him that any number of times before she'd left him—left them—two years ago. It was the one piece of her unending streams of advice he should have listened to, but he was always forgetting.

In seconds, his Lana and Tammy Cullen had hugged and were giggling together like he supposed a pair of fifteen-year-old girls were supposed to. Tammy dragged his daughter off for a whirlwind tour of the shop.

He slowed down a minute to check out the place. The dress shop felt welcoming and successful. Part of it was the thoughtful designer who had staged the store as carefully as the colorful designs. The other part was the surprising number of customers in a relatively small shop. Women swirled in and out of changing rooms, sipped tea while inspecting skirts and blouses. There was a happy buzz of voices from people glad to be there.

The stage manager at Emerald City Opera, Bill Cullen, had married the owner of the shop a year ago. Lana had hung out with their kids a lot during long rehearsals and shows, but he'd never thought to bring his daughter here. He could see that he should have. He supposed that a high-end women's clothing store was one of those "girly rights" that no one told single dads about.

Tammy was towing Lana from one display to the next. It was set up like a 1950s diner. Chrome and red leather booths were populated by mannequins in clothes hot enough to remind his libido that it had been a damned long dry spell. Single dads with young kids didn't date. There was never enough time and it got way too complicated the few times he'd tried it.

The girls slowed down at the wedding dresses and he heard their oohs and aahs despite the general noise level of customers chatting around the busy shop. Girls who were fifteen should not be admiring wedding dresses. Daughters who were twenty-five shouldn't be doing that. Maybe at thirty-five he'd let Lana out on her first date...like he'd have any say in the matter.

The shop manager, an elegant redhead, whisked past him in a dress that said, "I'm hot, powerful, and you couldn't handle me." She had a smile of welcome that invited and a ring that attested to the fact that some man thought he could, indeed, handle her.

"You're looking lost," she eased to a stop close beside him on a return loop.

"I'm with the blonde one," he hooked a thumb toward Lana sighing over evening gowns with low cuts that his daughter would never, ever, under any circumstances be allowed to even dream about wearing.

"It was so nice of your daughter to agree to be Tammy's model," the redhead sounded delighted. "We truly do appreciate you helping her out. However, it looks like they're going to be a while. If you want to wait, they'll end up in the back room eventually. There are places to sit there out of the fray."

He took one last glance around the room. He was the only

male present and was receiving the eye from several of the very well-tended women in the shop. That had been Lana's mother's trademark—he still did his best not to think her name—she was always well tended. And had finally found herself a sugar daddy who had offered to make sure she stayed that way—far beyond the capacity of the opera's chief lighting designer who had merely loved her.

"Yeah, that would be good."

The redhead guided him through the swinging doors to a diner's cook line that was filled with women's accessories. It was such a creative space that he had to slow down to admire it. Someone here knew what they were doing. Handbags dangled from pot hooks, pantries were filled with fine boots, and a walk-in freezer was lined in lush winter coats. The ceiling was hidden by dozens of inverted open umbrellas, splashes of color to delight the eye. It would be even better if they were backlit and the light shone through them—not his place to point that out. Still a very cheerful effort.

Another set of swinging doors and he was in a space that would almost put the opera's costume shop to shame. It was far smaller in scale, but there wasn't a wasted inch; it was a dressmaker's dream.

The redhead pointed him to a chair at a sewing machine, then whisked back to the shop while he admired the departing view. She might be too high-end and too married for his taste, but that didn't mean he was dead.

At the same instant a tall woman swooped in from the next room with her arms full of a gaudy mish-mash of fabric. Some of it looked like it had been graffitied all over, like girls used to do to their notebooks when he'd gone to high school. Now Lana stored all her school stuff in her tablet computer and he couldn't even check the outsides of her notebooks for doodles of boys' names.

She'd gone on dates; group dates, but even she called them

dates. It had taken him a lot of careful prodding to discover that "hanging out" was a bunch of people and that a "date" meant little more than that the bunch of people had an even number of boys and girls, not necessarily paired off thank God. If there was a boy in the next-level "going out" category, she hadn't let him know about it yet.

The woman dropped into the chair in front of the machine beside him.

"You applying for a job?" she nodded toward the machine he was seated at. Like the ones at the opera, it looked oversized and immensely complex.

"Not likely."

Then he looked at the woman. She was a knock-out in a different way than the store's manager. Long dark hair curled past golden skin. She was as shapely as the redhead, but because she was so tall it looked right on her. The redhead was more in a powerfully voluptuous category. This brunette was built…just right?

"Then what are you doing other than checking me out?"

He didn't fight the grin at her teasing tone. "Not much, I have to admit."

*ana stepped into the* back room and froze. There was her dad and he was…she knew that posture. Enough boys had tried it on her on dates. That laid-back pose with the "I'm so cool" smile. They always thought they were so charming and handsome, and most of them were just jerks.

Her dad was like the handsomest guy on the planet, except maybe Francis the track team captain. But what was he doing?

She grabbed Tammy's arm. "Who's that? She your aunt or something?"

"Kinda. We're not related. Kari just looks like me or maybe I look like her. Seriously though, she's amazing."

Lana couldn't believe that Tammy had asked her to come be a model, because Tammy always had the most incredible wardrobe. Every guy watched her walk by, not that she was so beautiful—though she was awfully pretty. They watched because she dressed like she was gorgeous. A lot of girls hated her for it; others envied her. If Lana got Tammy's help, maybe Francis would look at her that way.

Lana had known Tammy since right after her mom died and they moved to Seattle four years ago. As friends, they now had

Dad's divorce behind them and Tammy's new mom. Friends didn't get better than Tammy, but Lana still didn't like the way that Dad was looking at Kari.

"C'mon. You're like forever tall. I need to see how my clothes look on you."

Lana submitted, moving behind the screen to try on whatever Tammy had in mind. It felt weird changing with Dad in the room, but Tammy made it seem normal, so Lana did her best to calm her nerves. And peeked around the edge.

But her dad wasn't watching her.

# CHAPTER 4

*K*ari *only had a* distant look at the girl before she ducked behind the screen, but it was enough. The measurements that Tammy had given her had been good, these clothes should fit just fine. Rather than just leaving the fabric pinned, she dropped the dress she'd been working on under the sewing machine's foot and began running the seam.

"She's beautiful, Richard. She looks so much like you." His sleekly handsome-and-blond was transformed elegantly into her slender frame. She was a good choice for a model; a sharp contrast to Tammy's short, curvier frame and darker complexion.

"Scares the crap out of me every day," he rubbed at his face. "When she grows up I'm in so much trouble."

"Hello. Already grown."

He grimaced at her before slouching even lower in the chair and groaning. "I really didn't need to hear that."

"Oh," Kari did her best to sound contrite, "I mean she's such a cute toddler. Do the little boys follow her all over the pre-school grounds?"

"With their tongues hanging out. Have since she was about

three. That's the problem," his chuckle acknowledged he was being ridiculous, which she liked about him.

"What's the problem?"

"I'm a guy. I know what they're thinking at their age and I can't believe they're thinking it about my daughter."

"Bad news first or good news?" Kari appreciated the way he talked about his daughter, as if she was precious and worth protecting. Her own father, well, he hadn't made her feel the least bit safe. He'd never groped her, but his big-screen sports drinking buddies hadn't been so hands off. She'd developed early, both her body and her smarts, and rapidly learned to be scarce come half-time or seventh inning stretches or even long commercial breaks.

Richard looked at her through blue eyes shaded darker by an assessing scowl.

"Good news?" he asked cautiously.

"I'd say she loves you a lot."

"How can you tell? Did you even notice her?"

"I know, because of how long she was glaring at you for talking to me."

At his "Huh?" she pointed up at the mirror leaning against the wall behind the sewing machine.

"It wasn't me she was glaring at or she'd have spotted me watching her in the mirror," it had offered a clear view of Lana and Tammy talking.

"Perfect. It's not as if I have a love life for her to guard against anyway."

Kari had just assumed he was married, but saw there was no ring. She kept her thoughts about handsome single dads to herself. But it was hard. Perrin had married one just a year ago, had adopted Bill's two children, and would soon add a third to the family. Yeah right. And she'd known Richard for about three-and-a-half minutes. Stupid fantasies never did a girl any good.

"Okay, pretty lady. What's the bad news?"

"Sure you want to hear it?" *Pretty lady?* She rather liked that Richard was plain-spoken. Had he always done that, or learned it from his daughter? Teasing was fine, but she'd never liked games, and Richard didn't appear to be one to play them.

"No, but tell me anyway."

There was that straightforward thinking again. This time she waited until she finished her final seam and had clipped the thread.

She turned to face him fully for the first time. He was slouched low in the chair, but he was watching her face rather than her body. More reason to think he was decent.

"At her age…"

"Oh no!" Richard moaned and closed his eyes, wincing as if she'd just poked him with a sharp stick.

"…she's thinking along pretty much the same lines as the boys."

"Shit! I didn't need to know that either," he moaned.

# CHAPTER 5

*ana had kept an* eye out while Tammy went back and forth bringing her different clothes. The first couple had looked cool, especially the off-the-shoulder black-and-white zigzag top, but Tammy had rejected every one. A lot of them she didn't even get to try on; Tammy would just hold a killer blouse up in front of Lana, sigh and take it away.

Each time Lana peeked, Dad was looking less and less comfortable talking to the woman, which was good.

Tammy held up another, then took it away.

"Hey! That looked great!"

"Wrong color," Tammy insisted. "See?" She twisted Lana around to face the small mirror behind the screen. First she held it up to her own chest and it looked totally awesome. Then she held it up in front of Lana. It was good; it was hot. Francis would definitely look at her in it...but it didn't snap the way it did on Tammy.

"It's just because you're so different," Lana often envied Tammy her gold-skinned beauty. Their high school was in Ballard, a Scandinavian neighborhood of Seattle, and a whole lot of people were colored like Lana. And Tammy had developed real curves, Lana's body was so flat that she was barely female—at least it felt that way sometimes.

"No," Tammy shook her head. "You'll see, once I find it."

"I want to knock Francis off his feet."

"Then try this." It was the woman, Kari. Up close she looked as if she really could be Tammy's mom. Way taller, but the same Italian gold skin and real shape, just way taller—as tall as her dad.

Lana started to turn for the mirror.

"Don't look," Kari turned her away from it. "Instead, put it on and step out to show it to your dad. Watch his reaction. That will tell you more than your own."

Lana squinted at her, but Tammy stood behind her nodding.

She took the clothes from over Kari's arm. It was a dress. "I don't wear dresses."

"Trust her," Kari nodded at Tammy. "She's an amazing designer."

"Then what's your job?"

"She," Tammy slipped an arm around the woman's waist, "is the most amazing seamstress on the planet. I can think it up; she can make it so that it hangs great and actually fits people."

Lana shrugged. She was half out of her clothes before she realized that Tammy and Kari weren't going anywhere. She wanted to shoo them out, but already they were helping her. No one had helped her dress since her Mom had forced her into a stupid formal dress for a birthday party when she was six—the only one not wearing jeans, she hadn't been able to play in a single game. She fought against the bitter tears that apparently had no end. Stupid tears because Mom had only ever cared about how her daughter had made *her* look; they were so hard to stop.

Finally, she just closed her eyes against the pain and let them dress her in...whatever.

# CHAPTER 6

*R*ichard *was so desperate* for a distraction that he picked up a teen fashion magazine. Lots of young women wearing far too little. Ratted jeans, crop tops, wide brim hats. Some looked okay, but then he hit the brilliant red dress with too many cutouts and barely enough material to cover the model's butt. On the next page a girl who looked like she was sixteen wore a black bit of cloth with cleavage practically down to her panty line.

*No way in hell! Not his Lana!*

He tossed aside the magazine, shoved to his feet, and made it one step in Lana's direction before he stumbled back into his chair which almost flipped him backward into the sewing machine.

There she was—it was his Lana. He knew it was. But he barely recognized her despite that.

The blonde girl who looked so sharp in her black and white track outfit was gone. As was the sad girl, as devastated by her mother's abrupt departure as he'd been. In her place wasn't some under-clothed vixen. It was Lana, become herself. She'd blossomed into a version of herself he'd never imagined.

Her dress was the graffiti-laden fabric he'd watched Kari working with just moments before. It was purple, with pale-orange lettering that looked hand-painted. Quotes of great thinkers, silly faces, and words like: strength, passion, joy. It should have been garish—would have been if the shades and tones hadn't been so carefully selected—instead it was pure teen chic.

It hung loosely without hiding that she was lean and fit. Below a narrow belt that made a tight gather at the waist, it flowed to mid-thigh. No slutty tease of a neckline about to slide off her shoulder, the sleeves added a softness that countered the hard lines of her dead straight hair and tall figure.

Calf-high boots in a cobalt blue shouldn't have worked, but the tone matched the small purse slung low across her body on a thin strap and made her eyes shine. The only adornment, a thick copper bracelet tied her outfit together.

It wasn't sexy. It wasn't lurid.

But it also wasn't his little girl. It was a confident woman who was no longer afraid and no longer cowed by a mother's betrayal. Powerful in herself.

He staggered to his feet and went up to her, stopping half a step away.

"Daddy?" Lana asked him uncertainly. She hadn't called him that in a long time.

"You're...magnificent." He didn't know what else to say to her. Didn't know how to say how proud he was of her, so grown and so strong. So he did the only thing he could think of, he folded her into his arms and held her as tightly as he used to hold a little girl afraid of the dark.

He mouthed a *thank you* to Tammy who was doing a little victory dance.

Then he looked at Kari. She had her back to him, but kept wiping at her eyes, her hand coming away wet.

"*A date?*" *Kari grabbed* Tammy by the shoulders and shook her. "What am I going to do? Richard wants to take me out on a date."

"Cool!"

"Don't *Cool!* me, girl."

"Why are you so wound up? Do you like him?"

Kari dropped onto a stool. It was evening, rain pattered against the darkened windows. The store and studio were empty, yet still echoing with Lana and Richard's most recent visit. She and Tammy were the last ones here, waiting for Perrin to get back from her doctor's checkup.

"Well?" Tammy stood in front of her with her fists planted on her hips like a school marm.

"Can you tell me one thing not to like?" She waved a hand helplessly. Over the last few weeks, father and daughter had come in several times. Kari had watched them closely. And it was as if he was discovering his daughter all over again. Tammy had made Lana look chic, smart, sassy, modest, and amazing in turn, without once hitting what Perrin called the "Slut Button."

Throughout the fittings, Richard kept revealing facets of

how deeply he cared about his daughter's happiness. He hadn't cried when Lana tried on about the most amazing prom dress Kari had ever seen, but he'd come close.

Then he'd taken Tammy's hand and shook it with great respect. And when he'd taken Kari's hand, he'd asked her out on a date. She never saw it coming.

"Well," Tamara finally answered her. "Dad likes him. Jasp and I have known him since forever. Jasp worships him."

"Leave your little brother out of this." Jasper Cullen was way too smart about people for a twelve-year-old boy.

"Richard is really nice to him. He's always teaching Jasp lighting design stuff or letting him run the control board or something. I thought you'd like him. And he's a real hunk for a grown up."

Kari eyed Tammy.

"You thought I'd like him?"

Tammy's jaw dropped, but she recovered it with a quick shrug and a sheepish grin, though not very sheepish, "Oops!"

"So this wasn't about Lana? You set me up?" Kari felt an anger rising, but not very strongly. It was hard to be angry after seeing father and daughter together. After the last fitting, Lana had given both she and Tammy a huge hug before walking out holding her dad's hand.

"I gotta help Lana with Francis. You see, if I do, then she promised to get Tony to ask me to—" Tammy clamped her mouth shut, slapped a hand over it, and blushed so fiercely that her golden skin went several shades darker.

Kari raised her eyebrows in question, torn between horror and laughter.

"You can't tell Perrin or Dad," Tammy mumbled through her hand. "She might be cool with it, but Dad would freak."

"I'll keep quiet under two conditions."

Tammy nodded carefully. She was just as much a match-maker as Perrin. Kari had seen Perrin do it to others. Kari already had dodged a couple of Perrin's attempts. She didn't want to be set up, she just wanted to...meet the right guy. But she hadn't been watching out for Perrin's daughter; even though not related by blood the imp was equally dangerous.

"First condition, if anything happens with Tony that you aren't comfortable going to Perrin with, you come to me. That's not optional."

Tammy nodded but didn't remove her hand from over her mouth.

"Second condition, I have no idea what to wear. You have to help me. Deal?"

"Total deal! I already picked it out. C'mon," Tammy grabbed her hand and dragged her toward the front of the store.

Yep. A complete and absolute setup.

# CHAPTER 8

"*Why here?*" *Kari felt* as if she was crouching under the umbrella in order to disappear rather than merely to stay out of the rain. And she never should have let Tammy talk her into heels; she had to clutch Richard's arm to not go down on the wet cobblestones of Pike Place Market. Or had that too been Tammy's plan.

Oh no!

"Wait, don't tell me. Your daughter said something like, 'Tammy told me about this amazing Italian restaurant named Angelo's.'"

Richard's laugh was warm and welcoming, deep enough she could feel it rumbling about under the umbrella they crowded close to share. "I believe that's a direct quote. Why?"

Kari sighed and indicated for him to open the restaurant door, "It's a long story. I'll tell you over dinner."

They stepped in and Graziella greeted them, "*Ciao,* Kari. I didn't know you were coming."

Kari smiled back at the hostess. "Or you wouldn't have if Tammy hadn't already called you."

Graziella's smile didn't even flicker as she shrugged, "Oh,

there might have been something about saving the nicest table, the one that sits close by the fireplace. But I wouldn't know anything about that." She took their coats, which raised a whole other issue.

"Oh my God!" Richard simply stared at her.

The dress Tammy had chosen from the rack had been a simple drape of dark blue with a copper-red trim that accented lines and curves. It suggested and implied without revealing. It wasn't blatantly sexy, because somehow Tammy knew she wouldn't be comfortable in anything that was. But it certainly showed her figure to its very best possible form. It was a dress that she'd sewn dozens of for Perrin's customers, but had never thought to try on for herself.

Graziella winked and escorted them in. Richard took her arm to escort her...after stumbling in a very satisfying manner.

"You look amazing," his breath was a warm whisper in her ear as he pulled out her seat.

"I'm guessing that's your one suit, but you look pretty amazing in it yourself." She wasn't sure she'd ever sat across from such a handsome man before.

"Lady's smart as well as gorgeous," Richard was studying her face intently.

Kari wanted to brush at her hair, but Tammy had insisted she should leave it loose over her bare shoulders.

"I'm guessing you've been here before."

Kari looked around at the cozy Tuscan elegance. The fire was already warming away Seattle's damp evening chill. She wanted to wrap herself up here and never leave. The air was scented with basil and citrus and red sauce. The music was a bright Italian dancing tune, lively but soft enough to be comforting instead of enticing her to join in.

"My first time. This is a little out of my range. But we get together for these amazing dinners every week at the owner's mother's apartment. Perrin is best friends with the owner's wife and his mother." It was one of the true tests of a man or woman entering the "circle," how they fit in at Mama Maria's dinners. Kari expected that Richard would be as hand to glove.

"So," Richard reached across the table and took her hand. The warmth that spread through her didn't only come from the fire.

"You were going to tell me a story about a conspiracy involving two teenage girls."

Kari smiled, "You're clever, Richard Nyberg. Figure it out and I'll tell you where you go off track."

# CHAPTER 9

*R*ichard *didn't realize quite* how smart he was.
Not that first night when they had eaten
pappardelle and laughed and flirted.

Not the fifth night when they had tumbled into his bed and
both wept with the wonder of discovery.

His introduction to the entire crowd at Maria's had been a
huge shock and a wonderful one. Against his better judgment,
he'd brought Lana as well—that was when he learned just how
pointless it was to argue against a pair of fifteen-year-old girls
with a plan. He'd been overwhelmed, but he'd watched Lana
drink it in like a tonic. She needed family and friends—thrived
on it.

By the time he took both gals—his daughter and his lover—
back to Angelo's Tuscan Hearth Ristorante several months later,
he thought maybe he was getting a little wiser. And maybe his
daughter wasn't the only one who needed family. A whole
family, with a woman who truly wanted to be there for them.

He'd watched the bond grow between Lana and Kari over
Tammy's continuing fashion experiments. Richard had come to
enjoy the sessions when he could get away to watch.

Tammy's eye was very good, but sometimes it just flat out missed. Every now and then he'd be witness to his daughter the goof or the nerd—though Tammy thought that a few of the "failure" looks might work on another model. A couple of times the clothes had edged too far toward racy for his taste, but Kari had insisted these were safely conservative.

When he'd been dumb enough to argue, Kari had taken him to hang out by the parking lot when high school let out—thankfully not his daughter's so he could retain some illusions. Then she took him to a Nickelback rock concert with the two girls—and two boys who he hadn't counted on but rather liked by the end—and even those few vague illusions had disappeared. He'd stopped arguing with Tammy's taste level after that.

Lana had also taken to using the sewing machine beside Kari. Her first efforts were...first efforts. But she learned. She didn't have Tammy's eye, but she learned to sew, to fit, and, under Kari's tutelage, eventually to craft.

That was the unique thing that Kari brought to her work. She brought craft. That came from passion. And she had a passion that flowed through her work with Tammy, her patience with Lana, and the way she always shared so openly with him.

Tonight he had a beautiful woman on each arm as they arrived at Angelo's. The brightly lit ferry boats slid across Puget Sound looking like floating birthday cakes. He held the door and bowed for the women to proceed him.

Kari blushed and Lana giggled.

As he and Graziella took their coats, Richard could only marvel. Kari, who had revealed her casual side on most occasions, was once again dressed to kill. Instead of a classic simple black dress, it had been a simple, sleek red one—not racy red but a dark dusky red that offset and warmed her skin. Open neck, sleeveless, and ending mid-thigh. A copper bangle on one wrist reminded him of that first dress on Lana; he'd wager it was a Tammy touch intended to do precisely that. In this dress, Kari wasn't merely gorgeous, she was also as warm and welcoming as the Tuscan ambiance.

Lana was dressed back in that first look that Tammy had made for her. She was wrapped again in words of strength, joy, and—across the top of either shoulder—passion. He'd questioned that word on his daughter's body the first time. He didn't any longer. Her wrist bangle matched Kari's. The two women looked incredible together.

They sat back at the fireside table; this time he had been the one to make the request. It was a table for two, but it didn't matter—he took the third chair to the side with his daughter to his left and Kari to his right.

As close as family.

# CHAPTER 10

*Tonight was different. Kari* could feel it, and it wasn't merely that they were at Angelo's or that they were together. The three of them had eaten together dozens of times: at Richard's house, at restaurants, or huddled backstage at the opera among lighting instruments and cables when Richard couldn't get away for more than a few minutes.

Kari had found her hopes and her dreams, but she couldn't ask for them to come true. Richard and Lana were the family unit—something far too precious, too fragile to risk. It was in such perfect balance that she only dared sit on the outside and dream of being inside.

Like her clothing designs that had never excelled. She could breathe life into Tammy's ideas, create an exciting collaboration, but she couldn't go off on her own and find success. She was meant to be a part of something else, something bigger. But she didn't know how to get there from where she was.

"Kari," Richard's voice was a warm caress. It reminded her of how it felt every single time he held her, or she held him. It was hard to tell holder from holdee anymore; had been since the beginning.

His voice was also rough as if he was having trouble speaking.

"Yes?" She tried to take strength from the moment, but just as when she'd sat with Perrin the moment before she'd been promoted to help create Tammy's design label, the nerves were winning.

Richard opened his mouth again, but no sound came out. He cleared his throat. Sipped some water.

Lana rolled her eyes at him.

Finally, it was Lana who reached across the table and took Kari's hands which were chilled with nerves she could no longer hide.

"Dad will recover soon enough. I think it's kind of fun that women can have that effect on boys, don't you?"

Kari nodded, unsure what they were talking about. Richard affected her the same way; speechless with the wonder of the man.

"I don't want a mom."

And now Kari knew. It was a death knell that rang inside her. Those foolish family dreams that had been fluttering about in her head a moment ago, sank leaden into her stomach.

"But I could really use a friend."

"What?" The word stumbled out. She was suddenly feeling stupid.

"Having a mom didn't work so well. But I think you're great and once Dad recovers, he'll tell you that he loves you."

"Lana!" He managed a protest.

Kari glanced at Richard. She knew that look on his face. It was the look of seeing his daughter truly herself for the first time, or the shock over the scantily clad teens at concerts; the look of total confusion.

Lana didn't look at her father, but her grin turned about as wicked as Tammy's.

"Frankly, I think you two should have another kid, just the

way Perrin did. I'd probably think of her like more of a niece or something than as a sister, but I'd be cool with it if you decide. I just wanted you to know."

Lana let go of her hands with a final squeeze.

Kari was still trying to catch up.

And then she'd remembered Tammy's question when Kari had agreed to help with her clothing line. One word that had covered a world of hope and joy.

She turned to Richard who still appeared to be stunned speechless by the daughter who had inherited her frankness directly from her father.

Taking confidence from Lana's encouraging nod, Kari was the one to reach out and take Richard's hand.

"Really?" she asked as loudly as she could manage, which was little more than a whisper.

He nodded.

"Say you love her, Dad," Lana prompted.

He nodded again.

Then he clamped down on Kari's hand as if to make sure she wouldn't leave before he recovered his power of speech.

Not a chance.

Now that she knew where she belonged, she wasn't going anywhere.

# WHERE DREAMS ARE WELL DONE

*A place where food, fashion, and true love gather close by the fire.*

**Sam Walsh**, *cooks straight from his heart. Recently promoted to Executive Chef of a nationally-renowned Italian restaurant, he prepares to make his mark on the culinary world.*

**Luisa Valenti**, *his line expediter, trusts nothing. And whatever Luisa doesn't trust, she breaks.*

*But Luisa never received a gift like Sam's heart. Only together can they serve up a future Where Dreams Are Well Done.*

# CHAPTER 1

"*W*hat is wrong with you? I needed that fish three minutes ago. Did you learn to cook in a cave?"

"You needed it twelve seconds ago," Sam shot back. And decided against telling Luisa Valenti that she wasn't going to get it for another thirty seconds. Besides, the kitchen's aboyeur was busy dressing the plate of pappardelle with wild boar ragù that he'd just handed across the line.

"Fine, then where's my trio of sea scallops and squid-ink pasta?" She didn't even stop for a breath. "Though why everyone at a table would order the same dish is beyond sad. Just keep cooking the way you are and maybe we'll never see such dweebs ever again."

"Open your pretty eyes, Luisa," he teased her as his sous chef Marlys slid the three matching plates onto the warmer shelf that separated his station from Luisa's.

She rolled those beautiful brown eyes at him, making it clear that she knew he was trying to distract her from the laggard glazed halibut.

A glance down the cook line either way told him that they were running a little rough, but okay. He dropped another two orders of orzo into a pot of boiling water to help out Valerie. He also passed a tray of stuffed and breaded squash blossoms from Tony to Valerie as she turned to the deep fryer, saving her three extra steps she didn't have time for. He dropped the next two pieces of fish into pans for Marlys and accepted the two plates of sea bass ready for saucing.

He'd never have dared talk to Luisa that way while he was still a prep chef. He'd noticed her of course, there were only a dozen staff at Angelo's Tuscan Hearth Ristorante, including the three waitstaff, but his duties had mainly been in the morning before the restaurant opened. Angelo or Manuel would do the shopping at daybreak, then all of the proteins and produce would arrive for him to prep. When Manuel had shifted to Angelo's new restaurant, Sam had been pulled into the lunch line.

Up until this morning he'd thought he was just being trained to fill in where needed. Tonight they'd dropped him into the Executive Chef slot for dinner service because Angelo couldn't make it. If he had time, he'd be freaking out right now, but he didn't.

Over the last month he'd worked with Marlys, the grillardin, cooking the meats and Valerie at entremetier—the hot appetizers, soups, and pasta station, one of the keys to an Italian restaurant. He'd almost died at the sous chef position—keeping the saucier's eight pans always filled with whatever had to be sautéed to perfection, because Angelo accepted nothing less, which required being part magician, part juggler, and part octopus.

As a prep cook, the menu had been drilled into this head. Yes, it was always changing based on what was freshest in Seattle's Pike Place Market just out the back door. But there was a style, a flavor, a *feel* to Angelo's cooking that made sense once he understood it.

He'd even done some turns as the Executive Chef for lunch service. The lighter fare becoming second nature with practice.

That was when he first bumped heads with Luisa.

There was no way to miss Luisa's presence in the kitchen. It was the aboyeur's job to expedite service and did she ever. Luisa had every order in her head, never having to check a ticket twice. And she was very vocal about not getting everything in the exact order she'd called for it. Table Seven had a simple ragù, a pan-fried swordfish on a bed of angel hair pasta with one of Angelo's signature sauces that had to be made the moment before service, and a grilled lamb and baby asparagus with a Gorganzola cheese drizzle—and Luisa would throw a fit if they weren't all ready in the same five seconds even though they took drastically different amounts of time to cook. Actually, in the same three seconds.

But with Luisa in charge, there was never an undressed plate or a missed order. She was just as amazing as she looked. And as dangerous.

He slid across the missing halibut with a honey-rosemary-chestnut glaze and the accompanying bowl of the wild boar ragù.

"Finally!" she huffed at him.

Being the sole target of her ire was daunting. Everyone on this side of the cook line answered to him, but he answered to the fair Luisa.

He still didn't know how he'd landed in the Executive Chef slot through a dinner service. He'd entered the kitchen and Luisa had simply told him, "Angelo's busy tonight. It's your cook line." He'd taken his first breath about an hour into the meal, but hadn't had time yet to take a second one.

She finished dressing the plates with berry compote traced in an elegant line around the outline of the halibut. With immaculate timing, Graziella breezed in from the front of house, barely breaking stride as she gathered the completed dishes, and whisked back out.

It was a shock every single time to see them together. Two slender, beautiful Italian women with golden skin and lush dark hair that reached the middle of their backs. They could have been twins. Except Graziella was as gracious and patient as her name, unflappable under even the most dire circumstances. Luisa's heritage must be at least part Roman, as in Roman candle. Incendiary.

"What are you paying attention to, Chef?" she snapped at him.

Luisa hadn't looked up at him, but he'd been watching her and not his line and somehow she knew. A quick glance showed him that his momentary lapse to admire his aboyeur had just caused him more trouble.

"Fire three halibut and two sea bass, a lamb, a beef tenderloin, and two scallop."

Marlys grimaced, but hustled to get them all going.

It was too late, the next five tables were going to be all out of sync and he was going to catch hell for it.

# CHAPTER 2

*L*uisa kept her head down to hide her smile.

She remembered her first day here, Angelo and Manuel purposely messing with her, testing her. Angelo would finish a fish and then sit on it for thirty seconds just to break her rhythm. When she'd chewed him out over the line, he'd merely smiled and handed it across.

Manuel had mixed up three different orders, just to see if she'd catch it, like she was that dense. She'd ripped him a new one and he'd told Angelo to hire her on the spot.

That had been a year ago and Angelo's Tuscan Hearth Ristorante was now a well-oiled machine, reproducing the chef's magic to the table with class and consistency.

And at last it was finally turnabout, her turn to be testing someone else to Angelo's stratospheric standards. Manuel had left to run the new restaurant by the Seattle Center and Angelo wanted to focus on a third restaurant he was creating. She was the one who had suggested pulling Sam Walsh out of the prep role.

His prep had always been immaculate.

Then she'd spotted him making a quick lunch for himself and recognized the instinctual skill of his actions.

She'd spent three years in Italy studying restaurants, eking out every penny she could to continue doing so. Every three months she went to a new restaurant and volunteered to shadow and assist the aboyeur in exchange for food and a place to sleep. Many times she'd ultimately been offered a permanent job, but there'd been so much to learn, so many regional varieties of food, so many different chefs to study that she'd always refused. She'd worked her way from Rome down to Puglia, into Sicily and back up the west coast to Tuscany, Liguria, and the Piedmont before the money ran out.

She knew what a real chef looked like, even if Angelo and Manuel were too dense to notice what was in their midst.

When Sam had been momentarily called away, she'd snuck a forkful of his lunch and been stunned. No prep cook should be able to cook like that. Especially not a tall handsome one with auburn hair and such agile hands; he looked Irish not Italian for crying out loud. Of course Manuel was Mexican, but so were most of the sous chefs and line cooks in high-end restaurants throughout the U.S.

She'd stolen a second forkful, carried it over to Angelo, and fed it to him. His eyes had gone wide, then thoughtful when she pointed at Sam returning to his meal.

Sam spent some time looking for his fork, never spotting that she'd stolen it. It had been awfully cute.

But the fact that she'd been the one to discover him, meant that he had to perform even better than Manuel and Angelo did. If she had to hound him twice as hard to meet that standard, he'd just have to get used to it. And he had.

Until she'd distracted him.

She handed off the next order to one of Graziella's waiters and then did her best not to laugh at the cascading disaster his lapse had caused.

Luisa was used to men watching her. Hadn't thought much of it except when she wanted to take a likely candidate home with her. At least not until everyone started calling her Graziella's twin sister. When "evil twin sister" had slipped out of someone's mouth, she could only sigh in acknowledgment of the sad truth.

Grace and graciousness had never been in Luisa's genetic makeup; her "good twin" was elegantly second-generation Italian and Luisa was third-generation bitch. But that anyone thought she was that beautiful was still a surprise. And that Sam had noticed so much that he'd lost the thread of the meal...

"C'mon, Sam," she called out to distract herself. "It's your first dinner as Exec Chef. Don't drop the ball on me now."

He didn't snarl or glare at her. He didn't even frown. He simply turned to assist the suddenly overwhelmed Marlys trying to simultaneously fire nine dishes in eight pans.

Luisa moved down the line to chat with the patissier about a new dessert idea she'd had. She'd give Sam a little time to recover, but not too much.

# CHAPTER 3

*W*hen *the last two-plate* order had slid across to Luisa, Sam was ready to collapse.

Someone slapped him hard on the back and shoved a cold beer into his hand. A round of applause sounded down the line.

And across the cook line from him, even the bane of his existence was applauding with those elegantly fine hands of hers. He tipped his bottle to her in silent salute; they both knew he couldn't have done it without her help.

"So," Angelo and Manuel came in through the back door which had been left open to the warm spring night, "Let's see how you did." He took up the two plates of the final order and handed one to Manuel. A test? Tonight had been a test?

For what?

The two chefs tasted, chewed, swallowed, and then tasted each other's dishes.

"He didn't follow your recipe," Manuel pointed at the smoked eggplant and shrimp ravioli.

"No, he didn't," Angelo closed his eyes for a moment. "Walnut, no. Chestnut." He opened one eye to glare at Sam. "How much?"

"A single light grating over the eggplant before I smoked it." He knew it was taking liberties, but it had seemed right. Now he was less sure.

"Seems odd to me," Manuel replied.

Angelo harrumphed in agreement.

Sam was starting to get really worried, he knew chefs who'd been fired for tinkering with the Head Chef's recipes. Then he spotted Luisa's expression. She winked at him. After all of the abuse she'd unloaded on him during the meal, she winked at him.

Greatly encouraged, he winked back, then waited for Angelo and Manuel to get to the point.

"Going to have to change the damned recipe now," Angelo grumbled, but Sam could finally tell that he was pleased.

Angelo waved him out from behind the cook line. When he reached them, Angelo shook his hand. Manuel gave one of his quiet nods that Sam had long since learned was his form of high praise. Graziella had joined them by that point and kissed him on both cheeks before tasting some of Manuel's dinner and sighing happily. She slid an arm around her husband's waist and he held the bowl so that she could take another mouthful.

Sam felt himself wilting a little every time he saw them. Manuel and Graziella were so sweet together. When would he ever find something like they had? Based on results to date, *never* was his best guess.

"Looks like you were right, Luisa," Angelo looked at the aboyeur.

"Told you," was her pert reply.

"Told him what?" Sam asked.

But she just kept grinning at him.

"Told you what?" he asked Angelo.

"I think you two are ready to run this restaurant. Interested?"

Sam looked at Luisa and saw the stunned look on her face,

perfectly mirroring what he was feeling right at that moment. Well, something had finally put her in her place.

Angelo's Tuscan Hearth was top-rated as was the Piedmont Hearth which Manuel now ran across town. And not just top in the foodie Pacific Northwest, but nationally.

"We...*two?*" Luisa managed a bare whisper.

Her gaze slid to Angelo then back to him, her dark eyes gone wide.

Not to do this for a single night, but every night?

He tipped his head in the slightest question to her. Angelo was right, he couldn't have done it alone. But to run such a restaurant had been his goal since forever.

"You game?" he managed, his own whisper no louder than hers had been.

The astonishment shifted through a hundred stages on her beautiful face through consideration, weighing factors, acceptance, and finally a blinding smile that stunned him right back on his heels. He'd known she could smile...but not like that.

"Hell yeah!" was her verdict.

They traded high fives and a quick hug as the rest of the crew cheered for them.

# CHAPTER 4

*A*s far as **Luisa** knew, she and Sam had never actually touched, always separated by the width of the cook line. But his brief hug was warm and sincere. His big hands had wrapped briefly around her waist and she could still feel the impression of their easy strength. He'd smelled of the cook line; smoke and spice.

If she'd been seeing anyone, it might have had less impact on her thoughts. But she hadn't been. Not for several months, even before she'd stolen that taste of Sam's lunch. Then Angelo had assigned her to lay out his training because he was too busy with his plans for the next restaurant, and that had preoccupied her thoughts.

So, she'd made sure that "Angelo's" official schedule rotated Sam through every position until he could do each as well as the station chef normally posted there.

And it had worked. Worked beyond her wildest imaginings actually.

"Run the restaurant?" she whispered to herself, but it couldn't be real.

She cleaned and prepped her station for the next day, tossed out the sauces and garnish that wouldn't survive overnight, stowed everything else where it belonged. The other chefs were tending to their own stations. She'd demanded end-to-end ownership, if you needed more pans or towels or a sharper knife in mid-shift and didn't have it, it was your own damn fault. Angelo himself had been the slowest to adopt the change, but now agreed it was the best way.

"Run the restaurant?" She'd been aboyeur for a year, the longest she'd ever stayed anywhere, but that was a long way from running a restaurant.

She was staring at her immaculate station when a hand landed against the small of her back—she knew it was Sam's by the feel alone—and swept her from the kitchen and out into the main room. It was dark, the last of the diners were gone. The shadowed room was spotless. The tables already set with the lunch service cloths and tableware.

Only one table remained candlelit, the one closest to the hearth that was the centerpiece of Angelo's. The fireplace was a simple affair of stone and brass that anchored the room and gave it a lush ambience.

The table contained a chef's meal: a cutting board of crackers and several varieties of cheese, and a bottle of wine uncorked to breathe. Two glasses.

"You trying to woo me, Sam Walsh?" she asked as he held out her chair for her.

"No!" He startled as if she'd just whacked him with a wooden spoon. "Trying to be nice; sort of to say thanks for getting me this chance and maybe try to figure out what's next. Is nice too foreign for you, Luisa Valenti?"

He teased her. He'd actually teased her, which was quite a step for Sam Walsh. She considered several acerbic replies as he settled into the chair opposite and began pouring the wine.

"Way too foreign," she sighed. "I don't think that *nice* runs very deep in my bones."

He snorted out a laugh, "Might have noticed. Pity. However, they're such very *nice* bones."

She squinted at him over her wine glass, he'd chosen an Oregon Pinot Noir—her favorite Northwest wine. Luisa was starting to realize that Sam missed very little.

A part of her was offended by his easy agreement that she wasn't nice, even if most of her sadly agreed. But the compliment she hadn't been ready for.

"Now you're teasing me? Because I know that Sam Walsh never flirted with anyone." Which had stumped her at first. It was a standard part of her repertoire when trying to make male chefs behave. She'd had to find different buttons to push with Sam. And he was such a decent guy, she often fell back on simple cajoling. She didn't have a lot of experience with decent guys.

He slumped in his chair and rubbed at his face, "I'm so strung out that I must not know what I'm doing. Flirting with you doesn't sound like me, does it?"

"No, it doesn't. Why is that? Aren't I flirtable?"

# CHAPTER 5

*S*am *looked at the* Mona Lisa beautiful woman across the table from him; right down to the enigmatic smile. The candlelight played across her golden skin made it far too easy to imagine how *all* of her skin might look in such light.

He always felt oversized and awkward around her. And now? She was waiting for his explanation of...

He sipped at the wine. He'd noticed early on that when multiple American wines were circulating, this was the one Luisa always chose. He'd become partial to it himself. It had a fruity body and a low acidity that...had him thinking again about the sleek body and high acidity tongue that sat across the table from him.

"Well? Why haven't you flirted with me?" She did her best to sound offended, but she was also too busy looking pleased with their sudden change of circumstances to really pull it off.

And he was just tired enough to actually answer her question.

"I don't because I can remember every single thing about you since you walked in through that door."

"You what?"

"I was coming out of the cooler with a salmon almost as big around as you are. You breezed in looking like you already knew more about the restaurant than the guys running it. Turned out you did. Gorgeous, opinionated, and feisty as hell. Want me to tell you what you were wearing that day?"

She was looking at him with as much surprise as she'd shown at Angelo's announcement that the two of them were taking over the restaurant's operations.

"Forget it. Never mind. Let's talk about the restaurant," he took a large swallow of the wine. Should have kept his dumb mouth shut.

Luisa was continuing to eye him carefully. "No," she said it slowly, "let's talk about this."

Sam refreshed his glass, then set it aside because after everything else tonight, the alcohol was only going to make him even stupider.

"Talk to me, Sam." Luisa's voice sounded soft, uncertain—something he didn't even know she was capable of feeling until Angelo had blind-sided her with the offer.

Sam would rather—nothing came to mind. Climb the highest alligator? Wrestle the fiercest mountain? He was really exhausted.

"Sam," a flat, insistent tone.

"There's that tone," he acknowledged. "The utter surety of it. The woman who knows what she wants. Never thought you'd notice some lame prep cook."

"Of course I noticed you."

"Not really. I was just a lowly minion; not a chance that you'd actually see me. This was only supposed to be a damned temp job anyway."

"I—Wait!—What?"

"I was just back in Seattle for a few months. Spent a couple years in San Francisco at Acquerello. Then a year cooking for Batali in New York. Graziella got me the prep spot here while I figured out what I wanted to do next." Sam tried to think of some way to derail the story, but couldn't come up with a way now that it was rolling. *In the shitter now, boy!* was all he could think.

"But if you could do that, why did you stay here as a prep cook?"

"Yeah, good question. I eventually learned just how damn good Angelo was and realized this is where I was *supposed* to be. Watching that man build a sauce is a serious education; way beyond even my coursework at ICI in Calabria."

"You graduated from ICI?"

"Top of class," why was he bragging to her? Impressing Luisa wasn't something a guy was dumb enough to even try; she always knew what she wanted and just went for it.

"*Eventually,*" she drew the word out, "you were impressed with Angelo. But not at first?"

He shouldn't have said that either. He just shook his head and decided that the glass of wine would do more good inside him than it would sitting on the table.

"Because at first..." she was working it out.

Even shutting up wasn't going to do him any good. Luisa was too smart. He'd said too much. The moment he'd opened his mouth, he'd said too much.

"At first..." tasting it like a fine wine, half-lidded eyes, pursed lips. The way he'd always imagined she'd look in that half breath before a kiss.

"You sure it's not too late to talk about the restaurant instead?" But he knew it was.

Then he saw it click. Those stunning dark eyes zeroed in on him.

He shrugged, "Got me."

"You stayed because of me."

He nodded.

"Oh God. I really need a glass of wine."

"In your hand, Luisa."

She looked down at it in surprise, then knocked back a large swallow before returning her attention to him.

"It's not helping," she said as if it was his fault; which was probably true.

"Noticed that myself."

"Why didn't you say anything?"

# CHAPTER 6

*L**uisa was trying desperately* to make head or tails of what Sam was saying. But it wasn't working.

"I saw the kind of men who waited for you after work. Slick, urban," then Sam waved a hand at himself. He wore jeans, leather shoes battered and stained with too many hours in the kitchen, and a casual flannel shirt rolled up at the sleeves that had replaced his chef's jacket.

He was right; he didn't fit with what she'd always reached for. Looking the way she did, it was always easy to take almost any man she wanted off the shelf. She came from desperate poverty and kept picking some Mr. Rich-and-Successful. But they never seemed to fit when she tried them on.

"Did what I could to get over it. Then Angelo hooked me with his food," and again one of those easy shrugs of his powerful shoulders.

"And you told me tonight because you're—"

"Too exhausted to think before I speak." Then he glared at his half-empty wine glass. "I thought I was ready. Could handle whatever you..."

He cut himself off and looked up at her. She could see that the wine had nothing to do with what Sam was telling her.

"I wasn't ready for one thing," he continued.

"What was that?" She tried to guess. The hug had been nice, even promising. But if he was one of those guys who'd built a whole fantasy on such a brief contact, then he was in for a rude awakening. Life wasn't that easy.

"I've been cooking since I was six. Never wanted to do anything else. But I wasn't ready to find out that you believed in me. I'm still amazed that you're the one who saw..." he waved helplessly toward the kitchen.

Luisa knew she was in so much trouble. It wasn't the easy answer at all. Of course with Sam Walsh it couldn't be, could it? And once she'd seen him, and began tasting his food regularly...

"So I have a question," his voice was little more than a low rumble.

Was she ready for this? She wasn't going to just jump into bed with him because he'd...touched her with his answer. Of course, it hurt that he was right, she *would* have brushed off a mere prep cook. But the way he'd cooked tonight? That man, she couldn't help but notice.

For once not trusting her voice, she nodded for him to continue.

"Now that I've been dumb enough to drop that fat in the fryer, are you still okay running this restaurant with me, executive chef and aboyeur?"

At her nod of assent—how could she not find a way to make such an opportunity work—he sighed with relief.

"Well that's something, anyway," he mumbled softly into his glass.

It was clear that he was speaking to himself, so she did her best to pretend she couldn't guess what else he was thinking.

# CHAPTER 7

*or six long months it* was enough. A cool warm May turned into a cold November and they worked their asses off.

Their every waking thought was consumed by the restaurant. At first, Manuel or Angelo had joined Sam on the daily shopping expeditions in the middle of his night. The restaurant closed at ten, they were cleaned up and out the door by eleven, and except for a few fantasies about Luisa, he'd be asleep by one. Up at six in the chill, predawn darkness to get the pick of the market at Pike Place. Asleep from seven to ten—if he got back to sleep, and then into the restaurant.

Soon, he and Manuel had agreed to alternate mornings and do the shopping for both restaurants. But even on their off days, they were likely to bump into one another at the market, just seeing if there was anything particularly special that day.

Luisa showed up one morning, looking gloriously rumpled in sweatpants, a heavy sweater, and desperately clutching a large thermal mug of coffee. She was good, spotting some possibilities for the Daily Fresh menu that he'd missed. It was soon a routine to shop together and go out for breakfast afterward;

watch the late sunrise and the early tourists while someone else cooked them breakfast. He slept less, but in those quiet mornings is when he grew to know his aboyeur.

At first they discussed Angelo's. But soon they were discussing travels, different chefs and their restaurants, eventually they even wandered into past lovers. At the restaurant it was all business, but for the few hours between the shopping and the start of lunch service, that was theirs alone.

Luisa worked with Graziella on the restaurant operations. He worked with the other chefs and his prep chef replacement. In the second month he started running dish variations by Angelo, who was often found experimenting with a new dish on a small side stove. The new restaurant was going to be Southern Italian, a broad departure from the Tuscan and Piedmont themes of the first two, and that needed a lot of prep. Soon they were collaborating and testing dishes together; Graziella and Luisa offered their own insightful palates to the process of turning dishes into a menu. Sam had never so enjoyed the simple craft of cooking as those moments with Angelo.

At the end of six months, in the midst of a lashing November storm, Angelo sat the two of them down after closing and laid out a chart. He didn't need to say a thing. Rather than any dip in sales, there'd been a slow and steady increase. Angelo then laid down four new reviews that left no question he and Luisa were doing well as a team.

Angelo had shaken Sam's hand and kissed Luisa on top of the head before leaving them once again alone at the small table deep in the shadows of the closed restaurant. The silence stretched long after Angelo shut off the kitchen lights and left.

"I like that you still keep me on my toes on the cook line," Sam finally said to break the stillness. "Don't stop doing that."

"Deal," Luisa grinned at him. "Just don't stop blowing my mind with your new dishes." It was practically a caress that he felt right down to his heart. He loved that she loved his cooking.

After another overlong pause, it was Luisa who broke the silence.

"Do you think…" she trailed off.

"I don't know," he answered, fairly sure they were discussing the same topic. It had become like a live wire, or perhaps a tug of war across the cook line. The tension had built between them until he wasn't sleeping that much before the shopping trips either. They'd worked out such a deep cook line communication that it was, well, almost sexual. He couldn't think of any other way to describe it. It was sexual in every way…except for the complete lack of sex.

But would that blow apart their working relationship? Since that one brief hug, they hadn't touched so much as a fingertip: not in the restaurant, not while shopping, and not over breakfast.

"All I can think…" All he could think was how she'd look at the moment of perfect ecstasy and just how much he'd like to be the one to help her find it.

"Yes?" her voice was practically pleading with him.

"We have to try. Because if we don't…"

"…we'll both go stark, raving mad," she finished for him.

Sam could only nod.

Again the long silence—emphasized by a fresh lash of rain against the windows. His turn to break it.

"Not to sound crass, but…Your place or mine?"

Her smile quirked at that, "Mine is closer by about a block."

"All the difference in the world," he rose to his feet, and held out a hand to help her to her feet.

She looked at his hand, and then up into his eyes, studying him before she took it.

The shock was visceral, though not electric. Neither was it cooking-fire hot. It was simply such a powerful feeling of rightness that he didn't stop there. With the slightest tug, he kept pulling her in until she leaned against his chest, her head on his shoulder. He bent down to bury his face in her hair. Her slender form felt so perfect in his hands that he wrapped her tightly against him and simply held on.

"This had better be worth it, Sam Walsh."

"No guts, no glory, Luisa Valenti."

"I'm thinking…" she whispered.

"…that your apartment is too far away." And it definitely was.

A restaurant floor was no place to bed a woman for the first time. Then he remembered a luxurious sofa in the entryway, for waiting patrons—tomorrow's patrons.

He swept her up in his arms and carried her there. The soft light of the fire reached just well enough that he was able to see that she looked as incredible under her clothes as even his wildest fantasies had thought.

Sam made love to her while the rain storm rattled the front doors.

# CHAPTER 8

*L*uisa *felt thoroughly ravaged* and pleasantly trashy. They'd made it back to her studio apartment around three a.m. and passed out. The shopping alarm had gone off at five-thirty. They'd been half dressed by the time they remembered it was Monday and the restaurant was closed for the next two days. They hadn't gone back to sleep for a long while. The chill November rains gave them every reason to stay inside. So they did.

Now it was Tuesday mid-afternoon. Delivery pizza and Chinese cartons were scattered in among their discarded clothes. Damp towels from the most erotic shower of her life had been tossed on the floor as well. A shocking amount of protection was now in her garbage can hidden by a discreet Kleenex. And the most amazing chef and lover of her life lay draped across her like a man dead. They hadn't even gotten dressed—other than a quick robe for the food deliveries—in the last thirty-six hours.

Sam mumbled something unintelligible in her ear, rolled onto his side, then scooped her back against his chest and buried his face in her hair. He couldn't seem to get enough of that. He'd charmed her in so many ways that she could easily get lost in it.

She rubbed a hand along the back of his arm where it curled around her waist and held her tight. Her studio apartment had little going for it, other than a bed, a chair, and a dresser. It hadn't mattered to Sam. She idly wondered what his place was like. Did he have a masterful kitchen or did he care just as little for what lay beyond the restaurant as she did? No, Sam Walsh would have a one bedroom, maybe even a two. It would be messy around the edges, but the kitchen would be immaculate. He'd cook for her there.

Luisa didn't want to be charmed, not really. She wanted amazing sex and a challenging career. She had dreams, restaurant dreams. She knew how a restaurant should run—had learned an immense amount running Angelo's—and could easily imagine being aboyeur to a whole chain of them. But she couldn't imagine a chef-lover in that picture. Or at least she never had, which didn't make it any easier now.

Perhaps it didn't matter, her lovers never lasted long. They'd cross some line and she'd throw them out. Or they couldn't handle one of her caustic quips and they'd be gone.

Maybe that had already been dealt with. The blinders were definitely gone after what she and Sam had done to each other in the last day and a half.

"It's morning," she said even though the afternoon light—the first break from rain in days—was streaming in her west-facing window and warming the bed deliciously.

"Uh-huh," he grunted in her hair.

"So?"

"What."

"So, do you still respect me?"

"I," he nuzzled the back of her neck. She could feel against her backside that other parts of him were impossibly waking up as well. "I respect your sexual prowess no end. If I live through the afternoon, I'll upgrade that from respect to worship."

It was hard to argue with that. Sam was a perfect blend of gentle, creative, and sheer stamina. His body was built to order by any woman, but what he could do with those strong chef's hands of his had to be classified as pure glory.

Even as she gave herself to his roving hands and carnal intentions, she couldn't help wondering just how she'd be screwing this one up.

She knew it would be her.

Sam was far too nice a guy to take care of that for her.

# CHAPTER 9

"*Y*ou what?" *Sam strangled* painfully on the last word and grabbed his throat to stop himself from grabbing Luisa's right across the cook line.

"I got a job offer," she repeated more calmly than she ever called out an order.

Sam looked up and down the line. Marlys was staring at Luisa while searing a piece of mahi-mahi for table fourteen. He pointed to get her attention back on the fish before it burned.

Valerie, Tony, Vic, even Marko the dishwasher had all ground to a halt.

He looked down at the empty plate in front of him and for the life of him couldn't remember what went on it. He looked back up at Luisa.

"And you tell me now?"

She shrugged as if his world wasn't falling apart. They were practically living together. For six months they had been together every night, usually at his place because he had a kitchen and a decent sofa.

"Where?"

"L.A. at first; maybe Vegas and overseas after that. Wolfgang

Puck wants an experienced aboyeur to vet and enhance the operation of two of his high-end restaurants at the Bel-Air and the Ritz-Carlton. If that works out well, I'd expand into Spago and Cut."

It was the entire fine dining line with one of the leading restaurateurs in the country.

"It's just talk at this point," she finished prepping a plate and turned to hand it off.

But her timing was off; neither Graziella nor the other waiters were anywhere to be seen. It was his only clue that she was not nearly as calm or cool about this as she was pretending. Luisa never missed her cues, not once in the last six months since they'd become lovers had she eased up on pushing him for perfection in the kitchen. She'd also trained someone for Manuel and was helping Angelo do interviews for his Southern Italian Hearth over in Bellevue at the top of one of the towers.

"Just talk? You said you had an offer."

She shrugged negligently and he knew she was gone.

He wished to God he knew why.

He did his best to focus back on the service, managed to get the mahi-mahi with the right sauce and vegetables, even if it was on the wrong type of plate. He didn't change it and she didn't say a word before dressing it with a truffle oil finish.

All Sam knew was that there was small box in his pocket that had been burning a hole there for two days since he'd picked up the ring. And his plans to give it to her tonight, when they'd have the next two days off to celebrate, had just been charred past recognition.

# CHAPTER 10

*L*uisa hadn't been prepared for her own pain when Sam had shut her out. Not that she could blame him; it had been one of her least smooth exits in history. But this wasn't working for her. He was too close, too real, too important. She'd sworn no man would ever get in the way of her dreams. The Old Boys Club of restaurant chefs would never limit her options. She'd prove—

But the scar that she'd just sliced across Sam's heart was so visible; she'd never imagined anything that bad.

He didn't say another word to her. Instead he returned to creating perfect food like an emotionless machine. She hadn't had the heart to offer a single prod or nudge—he didn't give her cause to, except that one plate. His part of the service was perfect. Machine perfect.

As the last plated dish crossed the line, he turned to Marlys, whispered something to her, and was gone out the back door before she could think what to say. Marlys began cleaning up his station without looking at her once.

No one else on the line was talking to her either.

Luisa cleaned up her station amidst the echoing silence and retreated as quickly as she could.

She entered her apartment too weary to turn on the light. She also couldn't bear seeing one of Sam's forgotten jackets over the back of a chair or the silly mobile he'd bought at the Pike Place Market and hung in her window, made entirely of twisted vintage forks and spoons.

Two days and nights later she was still sitting in the dark when an envelope was slid under her door. She'd hurried barefoot to the peephole, but there was nothing to see and she couldn't bear to open the door. She slid down until she sat beside the envelope with her back to the door.

Inside there was a check. It was two-week's severance pay, plus an extra month's pay for bonus. Signed by Angelo.

A Post-it had been stuck to the front of the check.

Two words, no signature, but she'd recognize the handwriting anywhere.

"Good luck."

She caught the next flight to Los Angeles and wore sunglasses the whole way to hide her bloodshot eyes.

# CHAPTER 11

*S*am *finished the last* serving of the night and began cleaning up his station. He bantered a bit with Marlys; let the line see he was fine—after two months, he'd better be.

Graziella came up to him as he was finishing the cleanup on his station.

"I know," he told her. "I know. I'll put out an ad tomorrow for a new aboyeur. I just couldn't face doing it before. But I really want to thank you for covering, Graziella. You're amazing."

"I am amazing. Thank you for noticing."

He managed a smile. Her quick hug was surprising and kind.

She then nodded toward the front of house. "Someone waiting to see you." And she was gone.

Sam double-checked the kitchen. He was the last one, so he flipped off all except the safety night-light and pushed out into restaurant.

The lights were out. The fire was still going and a single candle burned on the table for two close. A lone woman sat at the table facing away from the kitchen.

For a moment he wondered how Graziella had circled

around so fast, but then he knew. His stomach clenched so hard that he couldn't breathe and had to hold onto the door frame to remain upright. He considered moving back through the door, but Luisa sat so still. Even the sound of the swinging door behind him didn't cause her to turn, as if she'd shatter at the least movement.

He circled the long way around the fire so that he didn't approach her from behind. Her face was as frozen as the rest of her. She was normally so animated that tonight she looked unnatural in her stillness.

Sam wanted to yell at her; spit out all of the hard hateful words that had rattled around inside him but never found any target. But the candle picked up the tracks of the silent tears that she made no effort to brush aside, if she was even aware of them. At a loss for what else to do, he sat down across from her.

He saw her swallow hard, several times, but he'd be damned if he'd be first to speak. If he was, he couldn't trust what would come out.

She nodded once, twice, as if trying to confirm something to herself, then began in a soft voice. Not quite looking at him, as if she didn't dare.

"My parents threw me out when I was fourteen. Boys and drugs and never going to school and crap like that was what they said. Maybe. But I know they also couldn't afford to feed me. I learned fast what cold and hungry was truly like. You get desperate real fast. Finally tried to hustle this chef coming out of a crappy restaurant. Offered to trade what I had to give for some food."

Sam wanted to close his eyes. Didn't want to see the hard memories that were crossing Luisa's lovely face, but he couldn't look away.

"Instead he fed me, helped me get a fake ID because I already looked like this, and gave me my first restaurant job. He paid me in food and a place to sleep on his floor. No money for the first six months because he didn't trust me to not buy drugs until I'd been clean a while."

Sam had heard stories like that. Except the offered payment was usually accepted. She'd gotten lucky.

"I don't have the palate to be a chef. But I'm smart. I earned my GED in two years even though I was missing four years of school. And I *saw* how restaurants worked; as clearly as a child's game. I cooked, cleaned, waitressed, did it all. But I was always fascinated by how all of the parts fit. How things flowed."

Sam nodded. He couldn't quite bring himself to tell her just how good she'd been at her job.

"I always dreamed of running a chain. That was my talisman, my Holy Grail. A big group of restaurants, making them function the way..." her voice stumbled and she took a deep gulping breath not far from a sob but continued. "...the way that *we* functioned. It was almost as good as sex. Better than, until I met you. Those months with you were the best of my life."

"Year," Sam managed the word without breaking his vocal cords.

"Year?"

"Six months after Angelo gave us the restaurant to run. And six more after we—" He couldn't finish the sentence.

"The best of my life," she repeated softly.

"Mine too," he managed because it had been true.

"But I didn't understand about boys...men. About you. I didn't get that what we had wasn't like anything I'd ever had before. I did the job. I worked for Wolfgang in amazing restaurants. And people listened. I *was* good."

"Best I've ever seen," Sam finally admitted. He didn't tend to think ahead, but he found himself trying to second guess this conversation. He wasn't having much luck. There was a thin thread of hope, but it was blended with the memory of a pain so intense that it was utterly blinding.

"I got my dream. The dream that a poor, desperate, cokehead

girl had held up as a light to find her way out of the tunnel. But I missed the most important part."

"What's that?" Sam held himself very tightly. Even daring to hope hurt almost as badly as the original wound.

"You."

"Me? Just that simply. Me?"

She nodded again, her arms wrapped tightly around her as if she was freezing to death sitting right next to the fire inside a warm restaurant.

"I'm just a dumb chef. You'd better explain it to me. Because last time I checked you're the one who—" He bit off the words. Clamped down on the recriminations that he wanted to spew all over her...because he didn't want to spew them any more.

For better or worse, he knew one truth absolutely.

He loved Luisa Valenti. God help him. Even just seeing her was—

He took a deep breath and spoke slowly so that he could choose his words carefully.

"We get back together and you're just going to wish you were back with Wolfgang's restaurants. And I don't want to leave Angelo's. He's perhaps the best Italian chef working today and he's given me his Number One restaurant to run. No way to solve that."

"There is. At least I hope there is."

"I'm listening," Sam hoped there was too.

At least a part of him hoped. He'd never wanted anything in his life as much as he wanted Luisa, but he knew that giving up Angelo's would only make him bitter. Same as if she gave up her dreams.

But most of him was still expecting the agony of the knife she'd rammed into him two months ago. He didn't know how he'd survive that a second time.

"Oh God, Sam. You're the best man there ever was. I can't believe you're even listening to me. I didn't deserve you."

Sam waited for her to continue, unable to risk more.

Impossibly she clenched her arms even tighter until her slender frame was shaking.

"I had the wrong dream."

"Say what?" That wasn't what he'd been expecting. He'd expected some plea for him to go with her. Or that she'd give up her own dreams, which he'd never allow. That's why he'd written the *Good luck* message even if he hadn't been able to bring himself to sign it.

"Angelo's was an amazing experience," he could hear the truth of it in her voice. "I never had so much fun. Angelo, Manuel, Marlys, Graziella, all of you guys. And that was before I noticed you. Then it just kept getting better. I asked to be busy, I asked to be challenged."

"And Wolfgang's organization does that for you."

"It did, past tense. He offered me consulting at Spago and Cut; flew in himself to do so. I thanked him and then I quit. I gave my two weeks' notice three weeks ago. I've been back for a week trying to find the bravery to come and see you."

"You *quit?*" Sam knew something was wrong here. "Because of me? No! That doesn't work. I won't let you—"

"It wasn't because of *you,* doofus. It was because of *me,*" she shouted him down just as she so often did on the cook line.

"Because of...you?" He was lost again. Then why was she here? To slice at him one more time didn't fit, even as he tried to brace himself to take it.

"Because of me," she said more calmly and unwound her arms, finally resting her hands in her lap as if too weary to do more. "I was too young and stupid to understand the most important dream of all, even if you knew it from the very first day."

"I did?"

She smiled at him; the merest reflection of the smile she gave right before she was going to unleash mayhem on his cook line just to tease him. The smile that also spilled forth when she'd woken in his arms to find him watching her. It wasn't much, but the memory of it was there.

"Yes," she continued. "I forgot to dream about being happy. I was happy with you, so God damn happy that I scared the shit out of myself and ran away. I'm hoping you'll give me a chance to try out that dream again."

"And I'm supposed to trust that?"

She nodded, but the fear was back and she hung her head to study her hands once more. It was so wrong because Luisa wasn't afraid of anything.

"How? Please tell me how I can." Because Sam had no idea—no matter how much he wanted to.

And when she looked up at him, the tears had returned. "Because I learned something new by leaving you that I never would have learned while we were together."

"What was that?"

"How much I love you, Sam Walsh."

And there it was. There was no way he could deny such a statement, especially not when it was so clear in his own heart. Had some part of him hoped that she'd be back? Was that why he'd never filled the aboyeur spot no matter how badly they needed it? Maybe so.

"Is love enough? You ran from it once."

"Hello. Young. Stupid. Already said that once not going to say it again." And there was just a hint of her glorious fire.

"You just did."

Her head hung once more as she mumbled so softly that it took him a moment to work out the words. "I'd say it a thousand times if it would fix anything."

Then he noticed the strangest thing. The agony that had been his constant companion these last two months was no longer trying to kill him. He'd never once in his life felt about anyone the way he felt about Luisa. And something that good didn't just go away.

"Maybe I was the stupid one."

"How's that?" Luisa glanced up at him sideways through that glorious fall of hair.

"I'm the one who let you go. I'm the one who didn't follow you. You were...everything. I was cooking for you, Luisa. From that first day, I was cooking for you even when I was the only one eating my food. But I never once thought to follow you into *your* dream."

"You idiot, Sam Walsh. If you're that stupid, I should have left you as a prep cook." She jabbed a finger back toward the kitchen. "You belong on *that* cook line the same way Manuel does. What you're doing here is bloody magic. Don't you ever dare doubt that or I'll come back just to haunt your ass."

All that fire and righteousness and pure life that was the secret recipe of Luisa Valenti flashed into being. The woman driven as hard toward perfection as he was shone before him, incandescent. And she wasn't done yet.

"Follow *me*? Me the idiot? I'd have knifed you for being that stupid if you'd so much as tried!" She thudded a fist down on the table hard enough that it was lucky there was no wine there tonight.

"But what's in it for you?"

"Other than being with the best man and best lover I've ever had?"

Sam nodded. He liked being those things for such an incredible, self-made woman. But it was the two of them together who had made this restaurant sing. It had been the two of them together that had given him hope and purpose beyond anything he'd ever imagined. She'd certainly left him with no taste for any other.

She turned just enough to glance toward the kitchen door. He could see the longing on her face. Could see the tears once more starting down her cheeks. It was impossible to doubt that she missed the perfect synchronicity of running Angelo's. Past speech, she flapped a hand helplessly to indicate the restaurant.

"We really did something truly amazing here," Sam had never been prouder of anything in his life than what they'd done together.

She nodded again, and the tears still ran.

"I've been trying to keep it to the standard you set."

"I've watched the reviews," she whispered.

"Hoping I'd fail without you?"

"Praying you'd succeed."

And he had. He and all the others had held the line for two brutal months. But...there'd been no joy. And it seemed that Luisa had found the same: incredible success, but no joy. Was that what he'd been searching for when he walked away from Acquerello, Batali, and all the others?

"Sam?" Luisa was studying his face but he had no way to guess what she was seeing because he had no idea what he was feeling.

"Was that the missing ingredient?"

"What missing ingredient?" Luisa narrowed eyes told him he wasn't making any sense.

"Joy." He almost laughed, but didn't because he was afraid he'd be violently sick if he did. "We had it. Together. I think we actually had it but neither of us was smart enough to see it. I never even thought about going with Wolfgang Puck."

"He's a smart man, you'd have had your own restaurant inside a month. But you *belong* here."

He tipped his head. "Without you? I'm not so sure."

"*This. Here.* This is where joy is. In this restaurant. With you!"

# CHAPTER 12

*A*nd then Luisa heard her own words. She lay her forehead on her crossed arms on the table to hide her shame. "Don't listen to me. I'm an idiot." It *had* been here, until she'd shattered it like an entire stack of dinnerware tumbling to a concrete floor.

"You're repeating yourself."

She raised a hand just enough to give Sam the finger.

He was right, she'd walked away from joy without even knowing it. And in doing so, she'd broken the greatest gift he'd ever given her, his trust.

Her parents hadn't trusted her. Nor that first chef who'd been kind rather than avaricious. Wolfgang had trusted her, or started to, until she'd broken that as well.

There was no way to fix this. She'd broken everything, just as she had her whole life.

Luisa stumbled to her feet.

"I'm sorry, Sam. I should never have come. I don't know what I was thinking. I wish you—" the words caught in her throat, "—Good Luck." Just as he'd wished her, and then she raced toward the door without looking up.

She made it two steps before he caught her arm. He stopped her not with some harsh grab, because there wasn't a harsh bone in Sam Walsh's body. He stopped her with the lightest of touches.

"What's your dream of the future, Luisa?"

Despite all her attempts over the last three weeks, she'd never thought about this moment. Of the moment just past when it wasn't a question of whether or not Sam would even talk to her. All she could do was shake her head; she had no idea. She looked at the floor but couldn't escape that light touch on her arm.

She could feel him rise and step in front of her.

Then his hand slipped into her hair and brushed it back over her shoulder. He'd always loved her hair. She'd thought of chopping it off when she was rid of him, so long that it was a real bother. Or maybe too much of a reminder. But she'd ultimately kept it because of the memory of how much Sam enjoyed it.

When he had it all brushed clear of her face, she still couldn't look up.

In answer, he simply pulled her against his chest, trapping her clenched arms between them, and leaned his cheek against her hair.

She'd already cried more tonight than she had in her entire life before meeting Sam. No, before *leaving* Sam. She hadn't ever truly wept until that night she'd cut out both their hearts and left them to burn on the cook line.

"So, you think you can just come back, pick up where you left off at Angelo's. As if we'd take you."

She shook her head. Of course they wouldn't.

"Then you figure you can just slide back into my bed."

"Well," she somehow found her voice, "I did let go of my apartment, so I do kinda *need* a bed to slide into."

Again she was being slow and finally heard his words only after she'd already answered them with a standard tease.

"Wait! What?" She pushed back to look up at him. He was smiling at her. The damned man was smiling. "You mean after that idi—"

"Don't say it again."

So she changed words, "—brainless thing I did, you'd actually take me back? That's even dum—"

He silenced her with a brush of his lips on hers.

For once, she couldn't think of anything to say.

"And after that, you're probably going to want the ring I had in my pocket that night."

She looked at him aghast, "You bought me a ring?"

"Uh-huh."

She covered her mouth in horror, "That same night? Oh God, I'm so sorry."

"Well we were practically living together and you had said you loved me."

"Yes, but then I—" Only while talking to Wolfgang about her plans for his flagship restaurants had she understood that, for the first time in her life, she'd meant it. Maybe she hadn't even understood it then, but that love had been enough to turn down Cut and Spago, and send her back to Seattle with no plans about what might happen. It wasn't a question of choosing, she'd *had* to come.

"Then you dumped me." Sam nodded.

"You really bought me a ring? I never dreamed that anyone would ever do something like that for someone like me."

"If you ever put yourself down again, you're going to piss me off, just so you know. And I *did* buy you a ring, doofus that I am. And even worse?"

"What's worse than that?"

"Even worse," he confirmed. "I love you so much that despite two months of trying, I still can't imagine a life without you."

Luisa knew exactly how he felt. "You're a very smart man, Sam."

"Not likely, I'm a chef." But she could hear the pride in that achievement.

She couldn't help herself. She giggled. Then it turned into a kind of inappropriate laugh that she couldn't stop.

"What?" he asked softly.

She went up on her tiptoes to give Sam a kiss seasoned with pure joy.

He was smiling as well by the time she settled back onto her heels. She grinned up at him in a moment of wonder before explaining. Somehow, this one time, life was serving up the perfect dish rather than kicking her to the curb as it so often had before.

"I was just thinking, what with you being the best man I've ever met and all..."

"What?" Sam's voice was as soft and patient as he'd always been.

"I bet you kept the ring."

In answer, Sam lifted her left hand from where it was still clenched between them, and kissed her on her ring finger.

Then he pulled her once more tightly against him and buried his face in her hair.

# WHERE DREAMS THRIVE

*A place where food, fashion, and true love gather close by the fire.*

*Tammy Cullen, fresh from design school, returns to Seattle because home is where nothing ever changes.*

*Except her little brother has fallen in love, Mom is updating her fashion designs, and the teen line she created is doing just fine without her. Inducted into a circle of fabulous women, her way ahead remains a complete mystery. Her one goal: design and fabricate a perfect Christmas gift for her soon-to-be sister-in-law.*

*But the sister-in-law has a brother that she was wholly unprepared for, and boat designer Andre Clayton has definite Christmas plans of his own.*

# CHAPTER 1

"Hey, Gnome!" Tammy threw her arms around Jasper's neck.

"Hey, Loops," he nudged her out of the stream of people coming off the escalator into baggage claim, then patted her on the back just the way you'd expect from a nineteen-year-old little brother, hard, with knuckles.

She hung on just to make him crazy, but he knew her games too well; he didn't even huff out a sigh. It made her so glad to see him that she could cry.

"Missed you, Loops." And it totally melted her that he said that. Of course, Jasper was like a people-genius, and would know that. Didn't matter, it worked on her every time.

"Hey, it's only been a couple months."

"Seven, but I'm so not counting."

Seven months since she'd been home? How had that much time slipped by so fast? She tugged at his collar-long ponytail before letting him go. It might have grown a couple inches. What else had she missed?

"You got any bags? Of course you do." He began leading them over to the wrong carousel. He almost never left Seattle whereas she'd been on so many planes these last few years that the world seriously needed to stop spinning.

She grabbed his ear and steered him the other way through the crowd. God, she'd missed being home so much. Even inside the airport it smelled different. JFK always smelled like it was about to sink into Queens, but SeaTac had that year-round evergreen thing happening because of all the conifers out here. And coming up Christmas, it was even more so.

"Many bags," she whispered in his ear because she always did. Even more now that she was finally coming home from design school in New York City—for good. "Presents!"

"Clothes," Jasp sighed.

"Duh! Fashion designer. Where is everyone?"

"They figured you'd have too much crap, so they sent me to fetch you on my own. Lucky me," he groaned it out. Then, unzipping his jacket, he turned to face her and pulled it open. It was the tailored shirt she'd sent him for his birthday. At least it *had* been.

"What did you *do* to it?" Tammy wanted to claw that grin off his face. She'd busted her ass designing that shirt. Used it to get extra credit in Advanced Tailoring Techniques, a 400-level class—before sending it to him. She'd gotten the A for the matching jacket that was going to be his Christmas present, so the shirt had kind of been spiking the ball in the end zone, but still!

It was the same shirt, elegant lines with just a nod-and-wink at hipster, but it was now a wild tie-dye way out on the neon spectrum instead of a chill off-white. It was actually an impressive job of the technique, but dammit, it wasn't her design anymore. And it sure didn't match the jacket any longer.

"I tie-dyed it."

"Not blind. *Why?*"

"Well I have this friend who—"

"*Female* friend."

His grin acknowledged that. Women flocked to Jasper like... honey didn't have it so good.

"She's a scene painter at the opera. Did a summer art camp thing for her niece's school. I was helping her out, but didn't have anything myself to dye."

"Except the shirt off your back."

"I think it came out great."

It had, but she wasn't going to admit it. No question but Jasp saw both sides of her reaction, too. But his grin wasn't going away.

"Summer? When was this camp?"

"July."

"You still seeing her?" She didn't know why she asked.

Roughly in unison they said, "The power of a great shirt." One of Mom's favorite sayings was *Never underestimate the power of a great dress.* Only fitting for one of the nation's leading fashion designers.

*That* was why he'd worn the summer-weight shirt to drive to the airport in December. Jasper's way of saying thanks, because she sure hadn't received more than a three-word text after his birthday: *It fits. Nice.*

"Or the power of taking it off at her summer camp," Tammy offered her best sneer.

"Not a total dork; I had a t-shirt under it. It was black, so no-go for the dye job." Making excuses wasn't like him either. Whoever art-camp-girl was had really gotten under his skin.

"You sure didn't wear such a nice shirt to a summer camp to impress the kids." It was weird for her to pull back mentally enough to really *see* Jasper as anything but her little brother. But she managed it this time. He'd been active at the opera since he was eleven working lights and sets. Their dad was the Stage Manager, so it had come about naturally for him. Jasp had gone full-time this year.

The demanding physical stage work had molded his body.

She always had his current measurements in her design book, but it hadn't really sunk in how much he'd changed over the years.

Tammy herself had taken after her birth mother and stopped growing at five-seven. Jasper had topped Dad's six feet by an inch. The year after Perrin had become their new mom, who was almost Dad-tall herself, Jasp had hit his first big growth spurt. Tammy had gone from being the mid-height of three to the runt of the litter.

Only Maxine, their Cairn terrier, was shorter than she was, which wasn't really winning much in the height competition. Her little sister took after Perrin and Dad; she was already the tallest girl in third grade, and would be blowing past Tammy all too soon.

Jasper had always been good looking, but when had he gone all handsome? The sweet-boy face all grown up and in need of a shave?

"She have a name?"

"Yeah. Amelia."

"She have a last one?"

"Clayton." But a strange look slipped across Jasper's face. She knew that face. After their birth mother's death-by-drunk-driver, and the four years until Perrin came along to become Mom, she'd raised Jasper pretty much on her own. That's what three-year-older sisters did even if she'd only been nine at the time. Dad had tried to help, but he hadn't been much better off than Jasper, until he'd met Perrin.

But on Jasper?

She *definitely* knew that face.

"You looking to *change* her last name?" It kind of slipped out before she knew it. She tried to twist it into a joke—did a pretty good job of it, she thought.

But his trademark one-shouldered shrug said he *was* thinking about it.

For half a second, she considered getting all serious about it and cornering him. He was pretty good at resisting for a while, but it still would be seriously fun to do because she always won that game. Then she thought about what Mom would do, and simply let out a *whoop!* loud enough to echo off the baggage claim ceiling.

People crowded close around the carousel jumped or cursed in surprise.

She threw her arms around him and hugged him hard.

"What?" Jasper struggled to peel her off until they were practically wrestling upright.

"I get to design a wedding dress!" She crowed it almost as loud as her initial shout.

That finally stopped him. His eyes went wide and a little desperate as the people around them began applauding, thinking Jasper had just proposed to her. She ignored them.

"Look, Tamara, even *I...me...*" he sputtered for a bit, "*myself* don't know anything yet. Okay? You gotta be chill about this."

"I swear," she did the seal and lock-her-lips thing, and a little cross on her forehead like they were burying the dead. It was an unbreakable vow between them. "Though I bet Mom already knows."

"No way."

"We're talking about Perrin Cullen here, Ms. Super Matchmaker. Remember she set up all three of her friends. Mom knows. She better not have started on Amelia's dress already. She's mine!" If she had, Tammy would take it hostage so that she could do it herself.

Too bad a bride didn't need two wedding dresses.

"How would you feel about wearing a dress at your own wedding?"

His eyes went from merely wild to panic. He grabbed her arm hard enough to hurt.

"What?"

"Wed-*ding?*" His voice cracked really impressively for a handsome nineteen-year-old. That *had* to hurt.

It was almost as cute as when his knees went out from under him, and he sat down hard on the baggage claim floor.

Because of his grip on her arm, she collapsed on top of him in a heap.

There was a lot of laughter, and calls to "get a room" among the crowd as she kissed him soundly—on the forehead.

# CHAPTER 2

*S*he checked out his photos on the drive home by the sisterly expedient of stealing his phone. Tammy didn't even need to grab his hand for a fingerprint unlock. She took a guess, and keyed in her own birthday. When his phone actually did unlock, she had to look out the window and watch the heavy Seattle traffic go by for a few minutes until her eyes cleared.

They were moving even slower than usual through the slush of a rare December snowfall. The snow was thick enough that the big orange shipping cranes of Harbor Island were barely visible, yet warm enough that almost none of it stuck. Typical.

Snow in the second week of December probably meant a green Christmas, because that's just the way Seattle was. The sky was darkening with sunset somewhere behind the low, heavy clouds. The city lights were becoming visible, but they wouldn't sparkle for most of another hour. Color *du jour?* Gray. Also typical.

His screensaver kicked in; it was the wedoption. Perrin and Dad's wedding with the two of them as Best Man and Maid of

Honor—the day Perrin had also legally become their Mom. It took a while longer before her eyes cleared after that one.

She unlocked her own phone and held them both up for Jasp to see.

"Yeah," was all he said when he saw the same photo on both. It was the moment that had changed both of their lives. Not that their lives had sucked at all, but they'd become way better that day.

Tammy pulled up his photo album.

"Hey, wait. How'd you get into my phone?"

"Duh!" was all she offered him as she began poking around. She didn't need to dig very deep; Amelia was suddenly everywhere. The two of them grinning like idiots in a montage of selfie backgrounds. She knew a lot of them: the waterfall up on Snoqualmie Ridge, backstage at the opera, at the Seattle Center's main fountain with crowds and musicians behind them (had to be the Bumbershoot Festival).

It was like a checklist of Jasp's favorite places. There was even one up in their family's favorite picnic spot. When Dad was too busy to get away during an opera production, they'd all show up with a picnic and climb up into a small loft built into the opera house ceiling. It was a strange anomaly, a work platform with a waist-high safety wall and a great view of the stage, six stories in the air. Sit down and it was utterly private. Picnics there was a tradition Mom had started back during their courtship.

Jasper had taken Amelia there, with a family-style picnic for two in the background. That was *major*.

The next one was even *more* major.

"You coughed up the cash to take her to *Angelo's*?"

"Yeah, why?"

Tammy wondered if the seatbelt would stretch forward enough to let her pound her head against the dashboard. Everything began at Angelo's Tuscan Hearth Ristorante. It had just gotten its second Michelin star, along with two of his other restaurants. Angelo had married one of Mom's best friends. Every courtship in the extended circle, including Dad's with Mom, had gone through there. She and Jasp had even been part of that.

This was *beyond* serious.

The sound changed as they rolled into the new highway tunnel under Seattle's waterfront. Tammy had to pop her ears and blink against the sudden brightness of the lights. Even the tunnel walls fit the day's color palette: concrete gray. Home-comings were supposed to be bright and sparkly.

And without such big surprises!

She stared back down at the photos, trying to figure out how she felt about all this. Jasper falling in love? He was three years younger than she was, so how was that even possible?

But in every photo, no matter how she searched, they looked crazy-close and stupid-happy. Either Jasp was super selective about the selfies he took with Amelia or they really were that gone on each other.

"She's beautiful." Darkly exotic, her face had such great lines. Hair almost as thick as Tammy's own chestnut mane, which flowed past Amelia's shoulders in midnight black and brilliant purple from the middle down.

"Yeah, she is. Some Senegalese, some Apache, a bit of French too, she thinks."

" 'Yeah, she is,' says the mush-boy. That's it, done with 'Gnome.'"

"Great! Unless I'm going back to being Troll."

"Nope. That was your kid's name. 'Gnome' was for the teen years.' From now on, you're 'Mush-boy.'" She never let him forget how staunchly he'd hated mushiness as a kid. He *was* just a male. She could easily forgive him but that didn't mean she had to let him off the hook.

"You know, she's got an older brother who—"

"No way! Tell me you are *not* turning into Mom."

That got his mouth shut.

"Besides, I've been back for like thirty seconds. Just give me a break."

Again, that one-shoulder shrug. Did it mean maybe he would? Or something more dire and she'd have to sit on him?

When he didn't say anything else, she let her attention drift to Amelia's skin tone. It would support almost anything, jewel tones, pastels, strong patterns... It wouldn't wash out like her own Italian coloring sometimes did. Those high cheekbones and that slender figure would let her get away with fashion murder.

Tammy wanted to hate her for it.

She herself was the only one in the family who had her birth mother's olive skin tone. Jasp had taken after Dad. Perrin, who she'd long since thought of as Mom without the slightest pinch, was a gold-blonde with the light skin to match (and a wicked lean figure) that she'd passed on to Cornelia. With the full figure, that Tammy had inherited along with her skin tone, she looked like the lone adoptee of the family.

Knowing nothing about Amelia except that she'd fallen for Jasper, Tammy stared out at the blank of the tunnel wall and tried to imagine what kind of dress she would want. Classic, racy, *avant-garde*? Please not the last. Tammy could do the runway over-the-top of *avant-garde* but preferred "modern" herself. Her first teen clothing line had been all modern before she'd left it behind to go to design school in New York. Auntie Kari had taken the line over. She would try to give it back, but no way. Kari had finally found her design niche, and Tammy so wasn't taking that away.

Besides, she wanted...something else. She wasn't sure what yet. But it was so close that she could almost taste it. Like...

She was snapped out of her reverie by their abrupt emergence from the tunnel. It seemed that during their brief passage underground, the day had finally found a new palette: dark—with sparkly accents. White and yellow building lights now twinkled brightly. Distant traffic lights added red, yellow, and green accents. Christmas decorations shone beyond either side of the highway like a cheery patchwork of rainbow dots.

Then Jasper took the first right turn immediately after the tunnel.

"Wait, where are we going?" He threaded his way back into town. "I've been awake for like three days straight: finals, graduation, packing, flights. I want to go home. See Mom and Dad. Sleep."

"Sorry, Loops. I'm under orders." And he pulled up to the curb and stopped at the head of Western Ave before it descended past Pike Place Market.

"No way." Tammy looked out the window, and couldn't believe what she was seeing.

"Seriously way, Loops. You're on your own from here."

The nerves shot through her. She knew who was there. It was… "This can't be real." Maybe she was so tired that she was hallucinating. But the engine was idling, the car heat was warm across her knees, and this was utterly impossible.

"Get out of my car already. I'll drop your junk at the house. Though I'll be charging you *beaucoup* for unloading it all."

"I lived in New York for four-and-a-half years. I got *stuff.*" Multiple internships had added the six months, despite her taking extra courses every quarter.

"Your stuff is my junk. Now go, before I put *your* junk in *my* Dumpster. I gotta meet Dad back at the opera. We've got a production of *Nutcracker* to get on the stage. Go!"

Numb, she gave him back his phone. Only as he was pulling away did she realize she was freezing. The slushy December night had fallen over Seattle and, while way warmer than New York, her t-shirt wasn't going to cut it. She managed to slap his trunk before he got away. He jerked to halt. Yanking open the passenger door, she grabbed her jacket, then slammed it again. Not fast enough, she still heard his taunt, "Bye, Loops."

She'd gotten the nickname the first morning that everyone was home after the wedoption. Tammy had been so ecstatic to have a whole family around the breakfast table for the first time in four years, that she'd poured Fruit Loops into her milk glass instead of the other way around.

Jasp had tagged her and it stuck; at least from him.

She stood perched high atop the north end of the Seattle waterfront. The towering office buildings to the left rose like flame-lit candles. The cozy alleys of Pike Place Market wended their way in between. She could just see the end of Post Alley where Angelo's was tucked away from the main tourist traffic flow.

More sparklies came from the waterfront Ferris wheel and the massive green-and-white ferries that scuttled over the pitch black waters of Elliott Bay, rushing commuters back to Bainbridge and Bremerton.

And directly in front of her?

Cutters Crabhouse.

It might be a Seattle Landmark, but it was also where all of *la Famiglia* legends began. *All* of them. Well, here and Angelo's Restaurant. But this was where all of the *women's* legends began.

Tammy had never quite figured out anything else to call them, using her birth mother's Italian, with an improper but totally capital F, *Famiglia*. So much more than just her nuclear family. "Extended family" didn't begin to describe it.

*La Famiglia* had started with Mom and her two best friends from college: Cassidy and Jo.

Mom's business partner—the still impossibly gorgeous model Melanie—was so super-close to them that they might all four have been sisters. And Mama Maria had raised Jo and Cassidy's husbands from diapers while she'd been a personal cook for a shipping magnate. Mama Maria totally pampered all four of the younger women.

For years Tammy had known about the Fabulous Five's "Nights at Cutters."

It was like the female mob: the Godmothers. They'd even done that literally. Every child born into the circle had four actual real-life godmothers to depend upon. The fact that she'd been thirteen and Japer ten when Dad and Perrin had married hadn't mattered. They each suddenly had a whole flock of Godmothers who always had their backs.

The five husbands, including Dad, had turned these nights into their own thing. They'd gather at different houses, drink, argue, play cards, go sailing, all sorts of guy stuff. When it was at their house, she and Jasper used to sit on the stairs and listen in. It was amazing how much these macho guys talked about their wives and kids.

That had been her childhood.

The last time she'd been home, she'd still been too young to go into a bar.

But now?

She was twenty-one and the Fabulous Five were waiting inside.

For her.

# CHAPTER 3

*O*nly when she stepped inside did she remember how she was dressed.

The bar at Cutters was perched high on the hill, overlooking a long sweep of the Seattle waterfront and Elliott Bay right across to the Olympic Mountains towering into the sky—or they would be if it weren't for the dark layer of clouds. Not that anything outside the windows really mattered. Cutters was *the* place to see and be seen.

And she was in the clothes that she'd put on *yesterday* after graduation. There'd been parties and dancing right through the night until she'd had to rush back to get her stuff and catch the plane. Plus a long rumpling flight.

She was wearing a dark red t-shirt with the TJPWC logo. Her youth line had been named for Tammy, Jasper, Perrin, and her dad Bill (except with a W for William so that his and Perrin's initials didn't turn into Peanut Butter). The C got tacked on when Cornelia joined the house—still not yet old enough to be told that she'd been named for being conceived on Mom and Dad's honeymoon in Corniglia, Italy. They'd honeymooned there because Cassidy had insisted it was such a wonderful village. The whole family had gone back twice since which had been only a little weird, knowing about Cornelia, but also crazy romantic.

It was one of the five towns of Cinque Terre, the five earths. That was her family, the Five Earths, plus Maxine the Cairn terrier.

But the Fabulous Five were completely something else.

Tammy brushed at her t-shirt. She'd custom-cut this one to her own figure. On the back was a sunshine-yellow smiley face and the words *powerful* and *confident*. The shirt always made her feel that way, and had been pretty successful. She'd even spotted it three separate times in New York and once during her year abroad in Paris and Milan. But it was still just a t-shirt and the words weren't delivering a whole lot of power or confidence at the moment.

At least these were her favorite jeans, large swirls of white and blue denim that curved down from her butt and wound around her legs. She always thought of it like the fingerprints of a giant who was holding her aloft.

And her muck boots. The streets of New York had been slushed out even worse than Seattle, and the boots wouldn't fit in any of her suitcases. The only place to carry them had been on her feet. Her hair wasn't brushed and somewhere along the way, probably wrestling with Jasper, she'd lost her last rubber hair band. No ponytail. No quick French braid. She was a mess.

Maybe—

Mom plowed into her from the side. "Tamara!" she squealed loudly enough to make Tammy's ears ring. And probably everyone else's in the room.

Suddenly none of that mattered. Tammy hugged Perrin as hard as she could.

She was here. This was home.

# CHAPTER 4

"$I$ still don't understand what you've been doing with your time. You didn't bring home a single boy."

"Mo-om," Perrin was backlit by the city beyond the window, and looked utterly amazing. The round of news, and drinks, had gone by quickly. It felt as if her sleepy brain had finally deplaned as well and she was all the way here.

All five women were dressed scads better than even everyday but, as always, Mom shone. It was a new design Tammy hadn't seen before but couldn't stop looking at. Her dress was a floor-length swirl of the entire rainbow that should look utterly ridiculous but instead wrapped around Perrin's slender frame in a way that made her look both elegant and sexy as hell.

"You know, if Dad hasn't already seen you in that dress, he's just gonna die."

"He almost did." And Mom's grin said exactly what had followed. Tammy definitely didn't want to be thinking about that. Parents. Having sex. Total weirdness.

"I didn't bring home a married boy either. Nor any girls, straight or not. Except this girl." Tammy tried to point at herself, but it felt as if she'd missed. She tried pointing at herself again with equally little success. She should never have drunk a whole Cosmo. A Cosmopolitan was Mom's preferred drink, a near-lethal blend of vodka, Triple Sec, cranberry juice, and lime that tasted like a sweet delight. Tammy's normal limit was about half of a hard cider, preferably pear.

Mom giggled. It was the greatest giggle on the planet, and she'd done it since they'd first met.

"Were there many *délicieux* boys for our Tamara?" Melanie rested her elbow on the table and her chin on her palm. Always conscious of her public image as a supermodel—and now almost a decade as the signature model and CEO of Perrin's Glorious Garb—it was the most unwound Tammy had ever seen her. Her straight fall of perfect blonde hair only reminded Tammy of the ruffled mess of her own chestnut snarl.

"None were as delicious as your accent makes them sound." She shrugged. "There were some good ones, but no keepers."

"She *is* only twenty-one," Jo hadn't even slouched as much as Melanie. She never slouched; always the serene, native-Alaskan, *gorgeously* curved lawyer. Also always the voice of reason in *La Famiglia*. That she was one of the most powerful women in Seattle was beyond cool.

"I'm going to snitch that blouse, Jo. I bet that satin-green would look really good on me."

"No," Mom polished off her Cosmo, signaled for another round. Then she waved a hand at the plates of appetizers and told the waiter, "More," without any other specifics before turning back to her.

The waiter must be used to them because she just smiled and went.

"Jo's wouldn't fit right. You should steal Cassidy's clothes; you're the same shape."

"No way." Tammy could only gawk. Cassidy had always been her own ideal of a woman's figure. Not lean like Mom or

Melanie who were like pre-designed for high-fashion attire. Cassidy Knowles was "everywoman" embodied.

"Thanks a lot, Perrin," Cassidy groaned. "Now I'm going to have to put locks on my closets. Did you have to be so beautiful, Tammy? I find it kind of depressing."

"Me?" Her voice almost cracked as badly as Jasper's had.

Mama Maria, who'd been watching her quietly just smiled and nodded.

Tammy could doubt all the others, but there was no questioning Mama Maria. Though they weren't related, they shared an Italian heritage—Tammy was often mistaken for her biological daughter. Though Mama Maria was technically old enough to be her grandmother, she'd aged too wonderfully for anyone to ever suggest that; not even when Tammy had been a teen.

Tammy knew she was pretty-ish. But for Cassidy to say that was...weird.

She definitely needed a topic change. "Where are all the men tonight? Jasp said Dad was at the opera."

Cassidy pointed out the window. It was fully dark now and she could see that just beyond the piers of Seattle's waterfront spread out below, ranged a whole array of multi-colored lights. They'd shown up without her noticing.

"The Christmas Boat Parade!" Dozens, tonight maybe even a hundred boats of every shape and size, scooted along the shore, each festooned with Christmas lights. Long familiarity let her pick out Russell's boat—her drink-blurred vision now offering her hyper focus instead. His fifty-foot sloop was a real standout for decoration, each year he and Dad had added something new. It was beautiful—artful rather than garish. She waved though they would never see it. So did the members of the Fabulous Five.

Of them all, only Cassidy was a real sailor—being married to Russell, she didn't have much of a choice. Jo had adapted as

Angelo was his first mate whenever he could escape his expanding empire.

For a bit, they caught her up on the news of Angelo's restaurants, Russell's growing success in nature photography, Josh's latest mystery novel, and Hogan's community work.

The arrival of more appetizers cut off that thread. She was slowly getting the hang of how topics flowed and shifted with the Fabulous Five. Especially as the alcoholic haze rose to wrap her in its warm cocoon. She had to sleep really soon if she was actually waxing poetic. Very bad sign.

But first there were pan-seared crab cakes, bison sliders, and ahi tuna tacos to be eaten. Another waiter added a fresh loaf of Cutters rosemary focaccia.

"I'll bloat," her empty Cosmo was replaced with a full one, "if I don't drown first."

"House rules. As long as we're all together, there are no calories here."

Tammy could only look at the lush spread and laugh.

"And," Mom raised her glass in a toast, "no secrets."

Cassidy practically snorted her white wine. Mama Maria laughed. Jo simply sighed as she thumped Cassidy on the back until she recovered. Melanie offered an elegant shrug of complicity—she and Mom really should have been twin sisters, they certainly acted like it, and came pretty close to looking like it.

Mom leaned close. "The real rule is that we never get drunk unless we're all together. But I like this one, too."

Tammy considered.

"Ooo!" Mom announced to the whole table. "Tammy has a secret. Tell us! Tell us! Tell us!"

Even Jo eventually took up the chant until the whole room was staring at them.

"Shush! I can't! I promised." She made the key-locked lips and dead-man-cross-on-her-forehead sign.

Mom laughed. "That's your and Jasper's sign. You mean Amelia."

Tammy grabbed her own head on either side of her face to stop it as soon as she realized she was nodding in agreement. She only noticed because it was making them all a little blurry, and there might be two of Melanie.

"I purposely didn't start her wedding dress. I knew you'd want to do that."

The reactions around the table weren't surprise, but rather about the rightness of Tammy designing the dress.

"But *he* doesn't even know if he wants to marry her."

Mom just flapped a hand at her. "He'll get there. Wait until you see them together."

"I saw pictures..."

"Then you know," Mom's glass was still up for a toast. "To the lovely couple."

Everyone joined in, clinking glasses all around, then drinking.

"And," Mama Maria's soft voice stopped them before their glasses were back down. "To the Smashing Six."

They all turned and toasted—her?

She wasn't just a visitor here tonight? Not just a homecoming? Even buffered by alcohol, the reality of it almost slammed her out of her chair.

Tammy was now part of *la Famiglia*. The first of the next generation, here among the Godmothers. She managed to get out of her chair without falling to the floor and circled the table hugging each of them in turn.

She didn't realize she was crying until Mom brushed aside her tears when Tammy slid back into her own seat.

"That's the last rule, we don't get to cry unless we're all crying." Sure enough, there wasn't a dry eye around the table.

# CHAPTER 5

*T*ammy was going to sleep the clock round until dinner.

At least that was her plan.

It was sabotaged by her body still being on East Coast time—and Jasper dropping Maxine on her face.

She and Jasper had picked out the little Cairn terrier shortly after it was born. It had been during the first time they'd had an outing as a family, before they *were* a family. They'd gone to the Seattle Dog Show, and it was totally fated to be. Perrin had brought it home after it was weaned, the evening before the wedoption transformed her into Mom, so that they'd all become a family at once.

When the terrier had settled from ecstasy to snuggle in her arms, she looked at Jasper over the oh-so-comfortable quilt she and Mom had made forever ago—a field of the pinks and golds of a Seattle sunrise, when the city's color palette wasn't being gray. He was sitting at the foot of her bed holding her foot. Whenever either of them was having a tough time, that's what the other did. Close, but not icky close.

Since her only problem was whether or not she'd feel a hangover if she sat up, she assumed this was about him.

"Spill it, Mush-boy."

He grimaced, "Got any lunch plans?"

"Lunch? I'd rather be sleeping." She snugged Maxine closer. "Don't bother us. We're napping." She closed her eyes like the dog's.

When Jasper didn't go away, she reopened one eye. He was just sitting there like a lump. Like he was asking something important. There was nothing important about lunch—considering how often she forgot to eat it. Another trait she shared with Mom. When a design had either of them by the throat, food, sleep, all of it went out the window.

But Jasper was...

"Oh. Sorry, sleep deprived. Got it. How soon?"

His glance didn't go toward the clock. Instead it went toward the stairs.

"You shit! Amelia's here? I'm a mess."

"It's just lunch. She's making sandwiches."

"When did you become an idiot about women, Jasp?" Tammy rolled her eyes. "Never mind. The moment you met Amelia is the answer. Let me guess, Mom and Dad are at work and Cornelia's at school so you could corner me. Go! Get out of here!" She kicked him through the sheets and quilt. "I'll be down in a sec, if only to rescue her from you."

"What? No. That's not what I want you to do. I want—"

"You idiot! Don't you think that she *knows* she's here for the sisterly stamp of approval? She's gonna be nervous as hell. Do not let her handle any sharp objects. Like, I dunno, cheese. Go!"

He went.

Tammy looked down at Maxine. "Sorry, pal. We're gonna have to get back to this later. No. No! *No!* Not the sad-puppy eyes. That's unfair. Besides, it's Mush-boy's fault, not mine."

She hurried for the shower because she'd certainly been too

drunk to take one last night. Her hair would have to wait for another time.

As she dressed and bolted for the stairs, the sad-puppy eyes still followed her from the cozy middle of his sunrise-colored quilt nest.

# CHAPTER 6

"*I*f you want to kill him, I'm glad to hel..." Tammy stumbled to a halt halfway into the big kitchen.

Amelia had dressed very carefully for the occasion. Upscale casual. Her makeup was so perfect that it was invisible—Tammy's was still packed somewhere. Her nails had been freshly painted to match her hair: not a single chip in the purple gloss. Tammy's were ragged and bare. Like her feet.

But that wasn't what stopped her—it was the man beside her. Unlike herself and Jasp, there was no doubting these two were brother and sister. The same lustrous coloring, the same face. He was Amelia's beauty and softness transformed. Not into big and macho, but—

And she was staring.

"I hope you don't mind, I brought Andre along for moral support."

"From me?" Tammy looked down at herself and couldn't imagine. "But why?"

"Because," Amelia waved a hand at her own clothes and Tammy finally focused on them.

"Those are mine." She must be really out of it to not have

noticed. "Well, mine and Auntie Kari's line. And...they look really good on you."

"I know. And that's the dress that got me interested in painting." Amelia was pointing at Tammy's chest.

She looked down at her clothes again. For lack of finding anything handy, and clean, she'd plundered the closet and come up with a more recent version of the first dress she'd ever designed. It was purple, and had been hand-painted in broad strokes with words like *strength, passion,* and *joy*. All closet rumpled, but at least it was clean. "No shit?"

"No shit. I was twelve when Mom bought me this supercool top for a school dance. It was one of yours, aquamarine with the long dark-honey lines."

"I always liked how that came out, and, yeah, I bet it looked utterly brilliant on you."

Andre nodded. Apparently it had.

"Then I looked you up online," Amelia continued in a rush, "and I saw that dress. I just had to have it. Mom made me paint the bedroom to pay for it—it really needed it. I kinda got inspired and painted one wall as a stormy sailing mural. Not a Winslow Homer, actually a mess, but I had real fun doing it."

Andre Clayton spoke for the first time. "Think she redid that wall about fifty-seven times." His voice was deep and warm, and she could hear that he'd probably helped her with every one. Maybe just cleaning brushes and mixing paints, but there was pride in his little sister there, loud and clear.

"That does it, Mush-boy," Tammy turned to Jasper who'd been hanging out on the other side of the island doing one of his fade tricks that let him be inconspicuous to everyone —except her.

Amelia was laughing out "Mush-boy?" in the background.

"Does what?" Jasper watched her with caution.

"You fuck this up, I'm gonna kill you."

He sighed. "That's what Mom told me this morning. Same words even."

"She already knew."

"Knew what?" Amelia looked a little wild-eyed.

"That—"

"No!" Jasper shouted but was on the wrong side of the island to move fast enough to stop her.

"—my mush of a baby brother loves you."

She did the old circle game, staying on the side of the granite island directly opposite Jasper as he scrambled after her. Bare feet on the wooden floor gave her good traction.

"Kinda obvious it's—"

She had to dodge around Andre who grinned as he side-stepped to clear the path, then eased back into Jasper's way. She could get to like him.

"—mutual. I love him too, so it's hard to blame you."

Jasper made a lunge directly across the island—he'd gotten a lot taller over the years and had serious reach—but, by flattening herself against the cupboards on the far side of the kitchen, she scooted clear.

"I can't even tease you that you could do better elsewhere."

And she was back where she started, facing Amelia.

Amelia didn't look shocked. Instead she looked ready to cry. "Can I hug you?"

"Hey, what are future sisters-in-law for?"

"Oh, my, God," Jasper's whisper was barely audible as they leaned into each other.

Amelia's hug was everything one could hope for from a new sister-in-law-to-be. But Amelia's brother standing silently behind her and watching them? Him she was less sure about.

# CHAPTER 7

*T*ammy caught the Number 28 bus into town, and enjoyed walking the last couple of blocks to Perrin's Glorious Garb. Mom's store had once stood on a dilapidated block of Belltown. Just north of the business core, most of the area had gone to condos and such.

It was in much better shape now, but Mom's block still had older shops, with unique stuff that couldn't be found in a hundred other places. The old Mexican restaurant where they ate lunch sometimes was still there around the corner. A bike shop, a jeweler, and a florist had the nearby storefronts. A used bookstore had opened that she'd definitely have to check out. They had a big section of vinyl and CDs as well. She'd dodged the vinyl craze but even a peek through the windows said that several of her New York friends would just die if they came to visit.

She hadn't seen Dad yet, but his text just said "Dinner" which meant he was super busy. Then he sent a line of heart emojis. Dad using emojis still cracked her up every time; usually he got it goofy-wrong. This time he got it exactly right. She sent back a goofy face anyway, then followed it up with even more hearts herself.

The boutique storefront was busy, so she only got to wave at Raquel who wore her ever-so-pleasant you're-going-to-walk-out-of-here-so-much-poorer smile. Brilliant red hair floating behind her, she also wore a power dress that Mom must have designed specifically for the store manager's second baby bump. It looked perfect.

The store's motif had been refreshed a couple times, but hadn't been really changed since she'd first walked in here nine years ago.

A 1950s diner of red leather and chrome. The Big Bopper was pitching *Chantilly Lace* softly on the sound system. The booths lacked tables, allowing full view of the seated and awesomely attired mannequins.

Mom's style had evolved. It stood out for Tammy after not having been home to see any new designs for awhile.

There was still the sexy vibe Mom couldn't help but load up on, but it wasn't so slap-you-in-the-face as when Tammy had been young. She'd found a subtleness that was actually a clearer statement of female complexity. Also, menswear had gone from one or two offerings to a quarter of the displays. And there was a spread of gender-neutral attire. Not that it removed anything, rather, it broke the past presumptions. Whoever wore it, no matter their orientation or preference, would look incredibly sharp. A trio of mannequins—male, female, and androgynous—all wore the same outfit, and each looked totally different.

That was Mom's eye. Her clothes made people beautiful, sexy, and capable.

Tammy's own teen styles had been more about confidence and playfulness.

She'd have to study what Mom had done here…later.

The only real change to the room over the years had been the door opening knocked through into the next building.

Perrin's Glorious Garb and TJPWC had bought out the old hardware store together. This side was Mom's, on the other had been her and Kari's.

Through the glass of the swinging door, she could see Taylor Swift rocking it on one of the big TVs. Perrin's clothes were classy and commanded the prices to match. Tammy had targeted the middle ground. Not cheap like she was a box store or anything, but not out of reach either. It was for the teens willing to push their clothing budget a bit, without having to break it.

And Kari had taken it further, crossing over from teen into New Adult without breaking the design aesthetic, as Amelia's outfit had proven.

No longer hers in anything except corporate structure, she didn't cross through to her old store. Instead she pushed through into the back room and caught Mom, Melanie, and Kari conferring at the table.

Mom and Melanie gave her hugs as if she'd been lost for years, rather than just out drinking together last night. Auntie Kari just clamped her arms around Tammy, and kept whispering, "Little Girl. Little Girl." as her tears dampened Tammy's hair. They looked the most alike of any of the extended family and friends. She and Auntie Kari had started close, and grown closer over the kajillions of hours spent bringing Tammy's clothing line to life.

They were both wiping their eyes by the time she shooed the three women back to their meeting.

For all of its success, online store, and warehouses, the fashion designs that had found such popularity all still came from these few women grouped around this table.

Tammy had interned at Wang, Givenchy, and Prada. Those were massive operations where the lead designer critiqued and built from what their staff created in hopes of striking some spark. Siriano stayed down in the trenches as did a few others.

Mom's vision, with edits by Melanie and Kari, was the heart and soul of every design from Perrin's Glorious Garb.

The big cutting table was covered by an expansive green rubber cutting mat marked in one-inch yellow squares. Cubbyholes of folded fabric now lined three walls instead of two. The hole that had been knocked into the back of the neighboring store to make a sewing room, had now taken over the entire shop except for TJPWC's storefront. All of the machines except Perrin's own pair, which took the short fourth wall, had moved next door as well.

But it was still the same room.

This was her home, even more than the house.

She'd created and run her teen line from this room.

Perrin's looks had walked from this room onto the pages of *Fashion Week* and the Paris, Tokyo, and Milan runways as high-end ready-to-wear. She rarely advertised; no need when even *People* did articles analyzing her latest shows. Of course, that Melanie had snagged a record-breaking sixth *Sports Illustrated* cover in one of Mom's swimsuits hadn't hurt business either.

Leaving them to their conferring—it looked all businessy, and while she'd mostly dodged the hangover, she just wasn't up for budgets and marketing plans—she began to browse the fabrics. Hers weren't here, they were next door. But there was something about these...

She fingered the stretchiness of a plum Jersey. Brushed a corner of daffodil satin across her cheek. Not her color, but it would snap on Amelia. However, it wouldn't have that perfect texture that would make Amelia *feel* like a bride. The tangerine crinoline made her smile, and the crackled brown leather reminded her of her attempts to update a classic bomber jacket. So hard to alter such an iconic image without just being derivative.

Tammy considered the mauve velveteen just to incite a reaction from Andre. Or perhaps a chartreuse neoprene for his sister's wedding dress would make him truly crazy.

He'd been impossible to read during lunch. They'd eaten at stools around the island, cozy, not bothering with the big dining table. Andre had only spoken when she'd directly prodded him, and his equanimity was even deeper than Jo's.

Not her kind of guy.

She plunged into conversations like they were an Olympic sport. When she'd tried to tease him, he'd pushed right back—done it well too, good sharp ripostes that challenged her. But each time she'd tried to escalate, he'd just smiled and wagged a finger, pointing at her and Amelia. It was *their* time to get to know each other; he was staying out of it. Not once during the whole lunch had he introduced a topic.

Amelia, on the other hand, was like the sister she'd never really had. Tammy loved Cornelia, but she'd only been four when Tammy had left for college. With Amelia, they were soon talking as if they'd been together their whole lives, but just hadn't met until now.

Jasper had still cardio-breathing-on-the-verge-of-hyperventilation for most of the lunch, trying to catch up with Tammy proposing for him. She'd have to remind him to do it properly; a girl deserved her moment.

Tammy fingered a frost-blue leather. Amelia would look really good in a bomber jacket made of that. Maybe as a Christmas present. She snipped a sample and moved along to an umber...no...a graphite leather for the trim and snipped another sample. Switch the two: graphite body, frost-blue accent. Yes.

"It wants a pop of color," Mom rested her hand on a magenta. Melanie and Kari had drifted off somewhere. Neither would think to interrupt a design-mode moment. She'd have to catch up with Kari some more before she left.

"No, the dark cherry."

Mom hesitated for just a moment, then tugged out a corner of the dark cherry for her.

Another snip. Tammy plucked a bolt of cotton similar to Amelia's skin color, and she laid the three bits of leather on it. She debated, then snipped samples in spruce and cedar. Amelia's eyes had just a hint of green in their brown depths— definitely the spruce. She dropped the bit of cedar in the scraps bag under the bench.

She set the spruce above the other three swatches.

"That doesn't quite work, does it?"

Perrin looked at her for a long moment.

"What?"

She slipped the scissors from Tammy's hand and took a corner off an obsidian leather, replacing the eye-color swatch.

"Wow! That pops. Weird, because this one is definitely Amelia's eye color," Tammy flapped the bit of spruce.

"For her, you want the magenta accent. But hers are not the eyes you're designing for. Spruce eyes get the magenta accent. Obsidian gets the dark cherry."

"But..." She could see the jacket taking shape, but not the person who'd be wearing it.

"Oh, honey." Mom hugged her hard.

"What?" She sounded like a lost parrot offering some nonsense syllable.

"I'm just so glad...you're home." Like she'd changed the thought midstream.

"Me, too."

Mom was sniffling, which started Tammy off as well.

"I don't ever want to leave again."

Mom didn't say a thing, she just stroked her hair like when she was a teen getting over her first heartbreak.

# CHAPTER 8

*Y*ou asleep?

*Not anymore,* Tammy texted back. The clock said it was seven a.m. Didn't her New York friends understand *anything* about time zones? Apparently not.

There was some kind of a conspiracy going on against her getting enough sleep. The whole family had sat up late last night just catching up. Cornelia had fallen asleep leaning against her on one side, while Maxine twitched happily with doggie dreams against her other one. Mom and Dad leaned together on the couch, and Jasp slouched in his favorite chair. How she'd left this for four-plus long years with only occasional visits, she'd never know.

*Breakfast. Out front in ten. Dress warmly.*

She sent back a, *K* because spelling *okay* was way beyond her capacity at this hour.

Tammy was three-quarters dressed before she came fully awake. One leg in her silk long johns and one out, she froze. That was a mistake; it sent her nose-diving to the carpet.

Seven a.m. Saturday. Nobody in the house would be up at this hour. The Cullens were *not* an early morning crew.

The message was from a number she didn't recognize. For half a moment she wondered if a boy *had* followed her from New York just as the Fabulous Five had suggested. Vernon? David? Then she saw that it was a local number, one not in her contact list.

Well, sitting on the floor in just her long johns wasn't going to answer anything. A peek out the window reminded her that her view was only the backyard. Jasp's and the master bedroom faced the street.

Out of options, she finished dressing and headed downstairs. Someone rousting her at this hour, they sure weren't getting her at her best.

The storm had cleared off yesterday, and the pre-dawn sky was brilliantly clear. In one of Seattle's quirky twists, it was already in the forties at this heathen hour, probably the fifties by midday. She'd roast in all these layers.

She didn't recognize whose car it was, but it was definitely her kind of vehicle. Low and muscley, and a classic. It was an immaculately restored 1960s Shelby Mustang.

Andre climbed out of the driver's side, and circled around to open the passenger door for her.

"What the hell?"

"Breakfast. You. Me. We're going to be related, might as well get to know each other," he continued to hold the door.

"At seven a.m. on a Saturday? Get a grip. I'm not even conscious."

He eyed the sky. "Should have been earlier, but that seemed cruel since you're probably still jet-lagged. Get in."

"Ordering me around is not a way to get me to cooperate." Then just to show him who was in charge, she got in. He closed the door just as she realized she'd gotten it backwards, and should have gone back into the house and crawled into bed still fully clothed to make her point.

He climbed in and buckled up.

She did her own seatbelt, then thumped her head against the headrest. "I'm so not awake yet."

He headed into town, "We'll fix that."

She wasn't going to ask how.

"Jasp really loves you a lot. Scared the crap out Amelia to meet you yesterday."

"Jeez. I'm just me. Not some *Friday the 13th* serial killer."

"Get that. Didn't matter. Why you two so close?"

"You know we had two moms?"

Andre nodded.

"Well, Jasper had three. I was his mom for four years until Perrin joined us."

"Hell of a burden for a kid."

Tammy just shrugged. She'd heard much worse stories among her college friends. "We were always safe and loved."

"It shows. Mom and Dad are like that, too. Always pisses me off when I hear about parents who weren't. You know, like deep inside makes me mad. I hear those stories, and I want to drop something damn heavy on their narcissistic heads." He didn't seem like the type to get mad easily, but she'd bet he was formidable when he did.

She really needed some hot cocoa or something.

"Jasper is great. You done good, Tamara."

"Only my two moms ever call me Tamara. Or Dad when I really make him nuts."

"Like the sound of it."

"Tough. You get me out of bed at this hour, you play by my rules."

"Sure, Tamara."

She sighed. Even Jasper wasn't this much of pain in the ass— not usually.

The Mustang's tires buzzed loudly as he rolled over the steel deck of the University drawbridge. Lake Union stretched off to the right, just starting to shimmer under the dawn light. The sun wouldn't climb high enough to clear the hills to the east for another hour to light the water directly, but Andre was right. Half an hour from now, watching the sunrise catch the water would be spectacular.

On the right side of the bridge, she saw the white top of Russell's tall mast; his boat was moored close by the east side. He'd mounted a small Christmas tree for the parade, complete with lights and decorations, right at the very top. It was beyond cute. Something she'd have to rib him about, if she was conscious enough to remember this moment later.

Andre then took the familiar right turn. Not a chance was she going to ask where they were going. But when he turned into the first harbor parking lot, she knew something was up.

"No way did you get Russell up at this hour." Cassidy and Russell were even less of morning birds than the Cullens.

"Nope."

"If you think my idea of a good time is going out on Russell's boat, you're wrong in so many ways." He parked, got out, and circled around.

"Not into sailing?" Andre sounded shocked as he opened her door. She could hear the morning honks of the duck family that lived around these docks.

"They're complaining about you bothering them at this early hour, you know."

"They're saying hello because I do this almost every morning. Besides, I bribe them mercilessly with bread crusts." He held up a couple slices of bread to prove his point.

"Fine. And I can open my own door."

"You weren't. How can you not like sailing?"

Against her will, her better judgment, and several other things she'd think of later, Tammy followed him to the dock. Together they tore off pieces of bread and tossed them to the waiting ducks.

"Because I almost killed Jasper the first time I ever went sailing."

Andre started to make a joke of it, then paused and eyed her carefully.

"Yeah, *for real* almost killed him." Still the single worst day of her life. She'd almost lost Jasper, driven away Perrin, and sabotaged her still-secret dreams of designing fashion—all in the same day. She managed to beg off most sailing trips since then by hanging with Mom and Melanie. Neither one was a big fan, though Mom had gotten over that day, mostly, because Jasp loved it so much. "I'm not getting on that boat."

"Then how about this one?"

An elegant sloop bobbed in the far slip. About a third smaller than Russell's fifty-footer. Like his car, she looked low and fast. And while Russell's boat might be a little rough around the edges, much like its owner, this one was immaculate. Beyond that.

"Yours? Next to Russell's?"

"Uh-huh. That's how we all met. Thought I was just hooking Amelia up with a chance to work at the opera's scene shop: Russell to your dad. Didn't know about Jasper until they were already an item."

He coaxed her aboard by promising to tell her Jasper and Amelia stories that she didn't yet know, which was totally unfair. No way could she resist that, and he knew it.

The sloop was thirty feet long and beyond perfect. Every bit of mahogany trim shone. There wasn't so much as a waver in a single line of the bright-varnished wooden hull or the teak decking. "You did a really remarkable job fixing her up."

"Thanks. Actually, I built her from scratch."

Tammy turned to study him. He was busy starting the engine, pulling in lines, and uncovering the sails. Each item was neatly stowed before he moved on to the next. It was the way she liked to design herself. She was an unusually clean designer.

Tammy had never understood how the clutterers could see their design and the images in their head when everything around them was messy.

He'd built it? That was a level of craftsmanship she understood. And it was far too rare, even in the advanced courses at design school. So many designers today thought of themselves as "conceptual artists", and assumed someone else would build their garments properly once they'd made it to the top.

She'd learned from Perrin that doing it right—yourself— gave you a real power. She'd learned so much from every single member of the Fabulous Five. If Perrin hadn't been such a great mom that she deserved the sole honor, she'd have called them *all* her mothers.

Melanie as model and business manager for Mom and her. Cassidy's Pacific Northwest wine collective was already surpassing Oregon and preparing to take on Napa. Mama Maria was still Seattle's best pastry chef. Jo managed the sprawling Pike Place Market and was on the board of every major arts organization in the city... And the Fabulous Five's husbands did no less.

She'd grown up surrounded by examples of doing it right.

It was clear that Andre had been raised the same.

"What's her name?" The boat had been moored bow-in, so Tammy hadn't seen the name across the stern. Then she looked at the boat's perfection. "Never mind. She's the *Amelia.*"

Andre eyed her. His silences spoke as much as Jasp's did.

"Your love for her just shines out of this boat."

He didn't bother replying. Andre focused on backing out of the slip, then turning for Lake Union. About a mile long, with the sun still just beginning to color the sky, it started as a beautiful sail on the quiet water. The city was still asleep—like any other rational person at seven on a Decembery Saturday morning.

Russell's boat always seemed so crowded and on the verge of

chaos—cheery chaos, but chaos nonetheless. Without the whole family crowded aboard, without Jasper here, she could feel her nerves easing off.

Being on a boat with Andre was a very smooth, controlled experience.

He handed off the tiller to her, as if he just assumed she could handle it, then moved forward to raise the sails. In moments, they were ghosting before the gentle breeze. The silence in the cockpit was deep when he cut the engine.

"You see things," he said softly after they'd eased down more than half the lake's length.

"Hello. Clothing designer. What's your excuse?"

"Hello. Boat designer." He pulled a bag out of the small cabin that he must have stashed her before coming to get her. He handed her a thermos mug.

She sniffed it carefully. "Hot chocolate not coffee."

"I asked." No Jasperish one-sided shrug with him. He was at ease with himself in a way she could never hope to be.

They slipped out onto the main body of the lake. Seattle towered to the south, Queen Anne and Capitol Hill to either side, and the green expanse of Gasworks Park commanded the north. At this lazy pace, they were ten minutes or more between tacks despite the lake's small size.

She could feel the nerves slipping off and floating away across the water. Not just boat nerves, but New York nerves, school nerves, and even homecoming nerves. This was really the first moment she'd truly stopped since...she had no idea when.

Watching Andre was a pleasant surprise too. He didn't pressure or push. He just...was letting her have her morning without being all weird about it. In between silences, he did tell some pretty funny stories about Jasper and Amelia—though she didn't trust the one about the three hamsters and the bicycle.

That one had almost made her spill her bowl of apple, yogurt, and honey all over the cockpit as she laughed.

He wasn't reticent, but neither did he waste a lot of words, almost sounding abrupt sometimes. But if she asked, he answered. It was almost a relief to not be second-guessing what he was thinking.

"What *are* you thinking?"

He watched her for a long moment. "I'm thinking I'm incredibly lucky."

"Why's that?"

"That for all the good things Jasper said about you, I'm starting to believe he fell short by some stretch."

Guys never flummoxed Tammy. Being raised by the circle of the Fabulous Five, she was hip to every come-on, cheesy line, and game men could play.

But if Andre was playing a game, it was one she'd never seen before.

If he wasn't, well, she hoped the heat in her cheeks was just from the steam off the cocoa.

# CHAPTER 9

"*M*om! Help!"

She must have sounded more desperate than she intended, because Mom dropped everything and raced around the design table.

"I haven't cut myself. It's just a clothing design emergency. I'm *so* stuck."

Mom huffed out a sharp breath, but looked her over anyway. Once she convinced herself they weren't racing to ER anytime soon, she threw her arms around her.

Tammy just held on.

"Hard to know which is worse, isn't it?"

At the moment, Tammy would vote for being stuck. She'd almost rather be racing to ER, because at least then she'd know what was wrong.

As a designer, this *was* the worst. She'd tried every trick she could think of. For two weeks she hadn't been able to get Amelia's jacket to come together. And, until she had that, Amelia's dress was impossible to think about.

Mom pulled out a pair of stools and sat down shoulder-to-shoulder just as they always had when working on a design.

"Show me."

So Tammy did. "Stacks of sketches. Half a jillion swatches of fabric. And a thousand ideas that totally suck!"

"Okay, first, take a breath."

Tammy did. "It isn't helping."

"Well, take another."

And while Tammy did, Mom gathered up all the sketches as if she was going to—

"No!"

But she was too late. Mom tore the first couple in half with a tear that jolted right up Tammy's spine until she thought her head would explode. "Want to do a couple?"

Tammy just shook her head.

That's how they'd met. The madcap Perrin Williams, tearing up months of another designer's work. Dad had nearly stroked out, because they were the only costume renderings he'd had for a new opera.

Oh...and she'd done it because they were terrible.

Then Perrin had showed her what design really meant. The costumes she'd done for that opera had been a total smash as well as turning them into a family.

"Shit! It sucks that I'm now in 'Carlotta Nightmare'-land." She grabbed a bunch and began shredding them until there was nothing left. Not wanting to do a major cleanup, she tossed just a couple pieces in Mom's face. Mom slipped a few down Tammy's back for old-times' sake, where they itched and crinkled until she managed to fish them out. The rest went into the trash.

Then Mom swept aside all of the fabrics except the original four. She snipped the dark graphite-gray and frost-blue into two pieces, and separated them in pairs. Next to one pair, she laid the magenta swatch.

"Make a jacket for Amelia out of just these three."

Tammy wanted to slap her forehead. The answer hadn't

been to add more, it had been to hone down. To edit. The one trick she hadn't tried, one of the very first Mom had taught her. "I can do that. Maybe."

"I know you can," Mom said in that of-course tone of hers. Then she bumped Tammy's shoulder with hers, before she walked away. She came back with a set of measurements on a Post-it, and placed it with the other set of three colors. "Make a complementary jacket with the dark cherry to this fit."

"But those are a guy's measurements. I want to make Amel—"

"Shush," Mom brushed her hair. "Trust me on this one, Tamara. You'll see it eventually. Do Amelia's first."

She already had Amelia's measurements in her design book —she'd taken them at that very first lunch. And she'd seen her often enough since that she really didn't need them, her figure was so clear in Tammy's head.

The two of them had met for a lunch on their own.

Then the four of them had done dinner together.

Even Jasp had gotten up in time to join in for a couple of Andre's chilly morning sails—he must really be in love with Amelia to do that. Only drenching rain seemed to break Andre's habit of rousting her at a ridiculous hour to sail. She'd also had dinner with their parents, and Amelia had dragged her to the waterfront warehouse where a sawdust-drenched Andre had proudly showed her the half-framed hull of his next boat—a custom job that he already had a down payment for.

Amelia might look like her brother, but she had a fun, quirky side that Tammy wanted to capture in the jacket.

Not even bothering to sketch, she began smoothing out the first chest panel. Curved lines, one of Tammy's favorite signatures. Yes. The hardness of graphite versus the softness of the mottled frost-blue like a cleavage, starting at...the lower quarter of the front zipper—but not low enough to be an arrow at her crotch. Then staying narrow. Not as an arcing race to expose breasts, but instead, making Amelia's face the top of a flower. The magenta, a slender seam between the graphite and frost to soften yet strengthen the arc. Repeated as a rose-petal trim around the collar.

Then...

# CHAPTER 10

*T*he living room was all Christmas tree, hot cocoa, and scones. Stockings along the bookcase, including a small one for Maxine stuffed to the brim with toys and treats because everyone bought something for the terrier.

Tammy had practically bawled on Mom's shoulder this morning when she saw it all. She remembered their first real Christmas together. Perrin had taught her to knit and they'd made stockings for everyone, covered with goofy pictures and each person's name knit right in. Not just some tube, but Mom had taught her how to properly rib the top, turn a heel, and shape the toe.

A decade of decorations were on every surface and dangling from every branch. Her first family had always decorated a small tree, and many of those were on the tree now. But Perrin had turned it into a joyous and bountiful celebration, requiring a much bigger tree to hold even half of the ornaments.

Each wearing personalized stocking hats and their Christmas socks, they'd opened presents together, taking the time to all appreciate each one.

Jasper went nuts over the tailored jacket she'd made him for

159

Christmas. He instantly raced upstairs to fish out the supposed-to-match tie-dye shirt. It still worked, just...differently. Instead of elegant, it was fun. Jasp had always been a serious kid, even before their birth-mom had been killed, though he was sharp enough to be funny, too. Amelia brought out the fun side of him. The crazy tie-dye under the elegant jacket was the new him in a lot of good ways.

She'd had to reach somewhere really deep for that design, and she was so glad that it hadn't been ruined by Jasper having the crazy idea to fall in love and tie-dye the shirt.

Mom spent a lot of time studying the jacket. Both up close and from a step back.

Her silent hug had tipped something inside Tammy. That as skilled a designer as Mom could like it that much was...perfect.

"Okay. Time for your real present." And Mom had fished the very last gift—a tiny box—out from where it had laid unnoticed behind the tree.

Inside was a key. "To what?"

No one would tell her. Her best target for info, Jasp, didn't know. Mom had known that he couldn't keep a secret from her. Dad's smile said he definitely was in on it, but it took days to wheedle her way past his shields.

He just raised his hands, "Not this time, Kiddo. Not even for the promise of your lasagna."

"Well, okay. I guess. I'm so glad to be home that I'll make us a lasagna soon anyway."

"With pumpkin pie, for New Year's Eve."

She hugged him. Dad had always been nuts in all the best ways.

With her key to...somewhere still clutched in her palm, they piled into the car, and drove down to Perrin's Glorious Garb. Mom's bright logo cheerily splashed across the door was the only brightness on the deserted street. There was even a thin slick of frost on the sidewalks.

"What are we doing here? It's Christmas. Besides, I already have a key to the shop."

Once they were all out of the car, Mom pointed to the other side of the street.

The old tattoo parlor had been resurrected several times over the years, but never lasted long.

For the first time in all the years, the glass storefront was clean. Several mannequins stood in the window, wearing only the simplest plain white for decency's sake, not style's.

They all crossed the empty street together. On the door, in simple yet elegant gold letters was a single word: Tamara.

Done up like it was a logo—as if she was Prada or Chanel.

Not TJPWC.

Not the whole family.

Just her.

Just—Tamara.

Numb, she slipped the key into the lock and opened the front door. Inside was a duplicate of the design room at the back of Perrin's Glorious Garb. A ginormous bow bloomed at the center of the sprawling cutting table. Down the side was an array of machines: a gorgeous Sailrite for heavy sewing, a serger, a Techsew for fine leather, and—

"No way!"

Mom slipped a hand around her waist. It was Mom's Singer Featherweight, the machine she'd taught Tammy how to sew on.

"I can't take that."

"Too late, honey. It's already yours. Besides, it's not really mine. In the beginning, it came from Cassidy's mom to me. It's time it moved on to you."

"But—" Tammy didn't even know what she wanted, what she was going to do. Yes, she could do anything here, but....

"For starters?" Mom could always read her moods. "Jasper, come here."

He came to stand in front of them, with a total Jasp frown of confusion. Mom reached out and brushed a hand over the front of his jacket. "Kari will want to commission this jacket for sale through TJPWC. If you age it up a bit, it's a must-have for Perrin's Glorious Garb, too."

Tammy couldn't even get out a "but" this time.

"And those bomber jackets you made. Those absolutely need to be a line. Different shadings, maybe even set them up as one-off custom exclusives without having to get crazy expensive. You know, 'Send us your photo and we'll tone the color selection for you.' Each custom, each signed. That kind of thing. I've always been good at the clothes, but you—oh God, Tamara, you make me feel so lucky that I've gotten to be your Mom—outerwear is so definitely your thing."

The bell on the front door chimed, and didn't stop for a while. The room soon filled with the Fabulous Five—no—the *other* members of the Smashing Six and their families. Everyone was trading hugs, oohing and aahing over the shop.

Russell and Angelo began popping champagne corks, and serving mimosas around the table. The kids got apple cider. Mama Maria had brought a massive box of her delicious cornetti.

It took a while, but Tammy managed to get Melanie and Mama Maria aside.

"For real?"

Melanie brushed a hand down her cheek, then, rather than a pair of air kisses, hugged her tightly. It wasn't something she did often.

"Remember when I picked your drawings out of all the applications to your Mom, not knowing they were yours?"

"The day I got permission to start TJPW. Even before Cornelia became the C."

"This," she pointed at Jasper. He sat on the floor across the room playing with Cornelia and the other kids. The four younger members of the Fabulous Five had given birth all within the same year. *"This* is more than I ever imagined was possible. Beautiful and perfect. *Très bon!"*

For just a moment she wondered if Melanie meant the design of Jasper's jacket or the gathering of family. Or both.

Melanie sighed happily before turning back to her.

Both.

"The other two jackets, Perrin showed them to Mama Maria and me already—you are *magnifique!* I would be proud to walk your jackets down the runway. Paired with the other two stores, it will be very good business as well."

No one knew the business of fashion better than Melanie, not even Jo.

She turned to Mama Maria.

Maria just wrapped her arms around Tammy.

That was all she needed to know.

# CHAPTER 11

"This is *your* thing, why am I along?"

Jasper was just looking pleased as he drove them to the Clayton's. "We had Christmas Eve dinner with Mom and Dad last night. I told Amelia we'd be glad to have Christmas Day dinner with them."

"It's the *we* part that doesn't make any sense." Jasper had indeed done it right. On one knee, nice ring, right at Angelo's restaurant where Cassidy had met Russell, and Angelo had courted Jo. Part of their own history with Perrin had been there. Melanie's too. It was only right that Jasper had gotten engaged there.

"Figure it out, Loops." From Jasper, who could always see everything about everyone—except himself and Amelia—that should have been a clue.

It wasn't.

When she went to grab Amelia's jacket from the trunk, there were two boxed presents there. "Who?"

"Mom said to make sure I grabbed the box*es*, plural. So I did. Sue me."

"But I only wrapped one. What's—"

Before she could check the labels, they were swept into the house.

It *was* fun. The Claytons were both software engineers, and had no explanation of how they'd had two such creative children. But they didn't enjoy them any the less for that.

Dinner was a blast, just as the prior one had been. She and Amelia ganging up on Jasper. Andre occasionally plowing them aside before the waters got too deep. A couple times, he'd teamed with Jasper to give back as good as he got. Their parents played half referee and half egging them all on.

But there was some undercurrent she couldn't put her finger on. Something going on that Jasper saw but wouldn't reveal. If she could get him aside, Tammy would get it out of him. But not in this crowd of merry bandits.

They gathered around the tree with pumpkin pie and hot chocolate laced with Baileys Irish Cream.

Jasper gave Amelia one of TJPWC's dresses which earned him a very serious kiss—after she stopped laughing. The laughter was explained when he opened his present of one of Perrin's lovely shirts. "I had to twist your Mom's arm to let me even pay wholesale." Tammy doubted if Kari had gotten a penny from Jasper.

Tammy decided two things. First, Amelia had great taste about what looked good on Jasper. And second, that the gift was also a little bit for her. Switching it out for the tie-dyed shirt, it would look great with the jacket Tammy had made.

After giving a big hug to let Amelia know she'd nailed it, Amelia handed her a small box.

"Please tell me this isn't another key. I don't think my heart could stand another surprise like that one today."

Both Amelia and Andre squinted at her.

"I'll explain after you open your present. I swore Jasper to secrecy so that I wouldn't spoil your gift."

"O-kay," Amelia waved at the box. "It's not a key. We didn't know what to get you, but Jasper said that you really like to draw. Not just sketch, but like pen-and-ink drawings. Andre and I went in on these together, but he picked them out. They're his favorite for drawing boat designs."

"I do love drawing." Something she didn't do enough of. From the box Tammy unearthed a trio of truly fine fountain pens in three different nib sizes. "Oh my God! These are so perfect."

Amelia looked very relieved.

Andre looked...satisfied? Like sailing—which he was slowly teaching her to enjoy—it was apparently a required part of their friendship that they had drawing in common.

Once she could force herself to stop admiring them, she picked up the first present and handed it to Amelia. As Amelia started unwrapping it, Tammy picked up the second box and read the label.

She handed it to Andre, but froze before she could let go of it.

"What?"

Tammy knew exactly what was in the box.

And now knew where Perrin had gotten the measurements for her to build to. *Not* one of the shop's models as she'd kind of assumed.

Mom had understood who her mind had been designing for in the very first instant. That's why Mom had hugged her so hard—for instinctively selecting the dark cherry leather over the magenta. At that moment, Mom had seen all the way ahead to this moment.

Tammy managed to release her hands, and just let it go. Everything racing out of her control.

Amelia and Andre pulled out their jackets simultaneously.

Amelia's looked just as great as Tammy had imagined. Everyone was commenting on it, and Amelia was hugging the thick sheepskin lining around herself.

Andre was brushing a hand along the smooth lines. Rather than a sweeping upward curve of the frost-blue that made Amelia look as if she truly was blooming, on Andre's jacket the curves spread out from his collar. They ran down his shoulders, forming arced points over his outer biceps. It made a strong man look invincible without, quite, tipping over into the super-hero vibe.

His eyes. She couldn't look away from his eyes.

Some part of her had known, even after that very first lunch when she'd chosen the dark cherry fabric. The accent color made his obsidian-dark eyes shine so brightly as they looked at her. And she didn't mind looking back one bit as the smile grew on his face.

Tammy now also understood the last thing Mom had said to her before she and Jasper had come here, "Never underestimate the power of a great jacket."

# WHERE DREAMS BEGIN

*Cassidy Knowles* has dreamt of going home since the day she left for college. Going home for Christmas is the last thing her roommate, *Jo Thompson*, wants to do. *Perrin*, the wild girl across the hall, has it much worse—she doesn't dare go home to her destructive past.

The three girls decide on a road trip from New York to Cassidy's family home in Seattle. The journey challenges them each in so many ways that it will either tear them apart or form a bond that lasts a lifetime.

# CHAPTER 1

## 14 YEARS BEFORE WHERE DREAMS ARE BORN

"*Y*ou can't be serious!" Cassidy turned from Perrin to Jo, the rational one of their trio. "Please tell me she isn't serious. We just drove forty-two hours to get here." They were collapsed on the living room sofa while her father made them hot cocoa. Every muscle ached from being cramped into the car for so long. Well, she and Jo were collapsed, Perrin was on the move like she was a ping-pong ball bouncing off the walls.

"It's Christmas!" Perrin never gave Jo a chance to answer. "What's the point of coming all the way to Seattle if I don't get to sit in Santa's lap. You told me about how much you loved that when you were a little girl, you hussy." Her happy smile made it impossible to take offense and, that she unleashed it all in a single breath, equally impossible to interrupt. "Santa's lap at the Bon Marché downtown. I'm sooo there. We're going, right after lunch."

Jo shrugged in resignation. One thing Cassidy and Jo had both learned since the first day they'd arrived at Vassar College was that Perrin was unstoppable.

Cassidy had gone to college in Poughkeepsie, New York, not

because it was as far as she could get from her father's meager winery on Bainbridge Island, Washington. That distance almost broke her heart. She did it because her mom, who had died when Cassidy was five, had gone there.

To land in the same place, however, Jo *had* run as far as she could from Ketchikan, Alaska. College housing probably thought Washington State and Alaska made them next-door neighbors and had housed them together.

As they'd sat on their twin beds the first day, carefully getting to know each other, a wild girl with apple-green hair had bombed into their room from hers across the hall. She and Jo had later agreed that there'd been no other word for it than "bombed"—a word they were to learn described most of the neighbor's actions.

The girl vibrated with energy and had blue eyes that were so big on her slender face that she looked like a manga character. The green hair falling in a lush wave down to her waist had turned out to be a wig—shoulder-length cotton-candy-pink hair that was not a wig kept sliding into view.

"Oh, my Gawd! Since when are chemistry majors *so dull,*" she'd turned back to shout the last across the hall through the open door she'd just come through. Without pausing for an answer she'd whirled back. "Please, please, please tell me that you two aren't chemistry majors."

"Pre-law," Jo had said in her soft voice.

Cassidy didn't know for sure. "Um, marketing. I think."

"I'm psych or art or maybe just humanities, do they have humanities here? Never mind. You're both perfect! And the three of us together? Whoo! Smoking hot. Boys are just gonna die at our feet. Come on! Let's go find a party." And she'd dragged them out of their room before they'd even finished unpacking.

As unlikely as it seemed on the first day of college, their neighbor from across the hall *had* found a party and was soon at the center of it. They were to quickly discover that if there weren't any parties, one just spontaneously combusted into existence around her—another aspect of a the girl's "bomb" ability. She could stroll into their room on a quiet Tuesday as they both studied at their desks, and three minutes later the room would be so crowded Cassidy couldn't breathe.

It also took a while to find out her name because it kept changing. It was Karen, Perrin's "boring" chemistry-major roommate, who informed her that they were all *Star Trek* characters. Which didn't tell Cassidy or Jo much.

The next time she gave a name, it was Perrin. Her name kept changing for everyone else, but after that and forever more she and Jo only called her Perrin. Apparently the second wife of an alien named Sarek, though she was a human from Earth.

"I don't know," Jo had offered one of her rare jokes later that night as the two of them lay in opposite beds. "If ever there was an alien attending Vassar, it's a reasonable postulation that Perrin is indeed that alien."

"The disguise is a little shaky," Cassidy had agreed and they'd shared a soft laugh.

Cassidy eventually observed that, while it wasn't an unreasonable conclusion, every now and then Perrin's frantic facade would slip. During those brief flashes, Cassidy glimpsed the terrified woman behind the dazzle and never had the heart to turn her away after that.

By Halloween, everyone recognized them as a trio. By Thanksgiving, they often received confused reactions if they weren't all together outside of classes.

And by the start of the three-week Christmas break, Cassidy had learned one more thing about her new friends. She herself was desperately homesick, but neither of them wanted to go home again—ever.

Jo looked ill when Cassidy had even asked if she was going back to Alaska.

And Perrin?

Home was the one topic she couldn't make jokes about. It was like a light switch. At the merest mention, the terror bloomed in Perrin's wide eyes, making her shrink and even cower.

When Cassidy had suggested that they split gas costs and road trip together to her father's winery, they'd practically tackled her in their joy. Actually, Perrin had—crashing Cassidy back onto the dorm room's small couch and kissing her soundly. The first, and hopefully last, time she was ever kissed by another girl.

Then Perrin had whispered so quietly against Cassidy's ear that she couldn't be sure she heard it right. "You're the best friend in world, Cassidy. My *first-ever* and bestest friend."

So, if mere hours after driving all of the way across the country Perrin wanted to go into Seattle and flirt with Santa, it was beyond Cassidy's power to stop her.

## CHAPTER 2

"What was that about? Why the rush?" Cassidy wanted to know.

"Let's go see the view," Perrin hurried out the bow doors on the ferry to face into the wind as it pulled out of Bainbridge Island Harbor beneath the golden sunset.

Cassidy and Jo, on the verge of settling into seats followed her.

Perrin didn't have a clue why she'd been so insistent. She didn't think about her actions, she just did them. Cassidy was the deep thinker of their trio. Maybe Jo too. Which left her, again, out in the wind.

Despite the December chill, she dragged Cassidy and Jo out onto the upper deck of the Bainbridge-to-Seattle ferry even as it left the Bainbridge dock. It was such a relief to be away from any direct connection to Cassidy's house. But the ferry was almost as bad, it held hundreds of cars and thousands of passengers. And all of them were so…happy.

She stood with her face into the wind. She'd thought that Vassar was as different as you could get from a South Jersey trailer park, and it was in a lot of ways. But *this?* Even crossing the whole country in two days hadn't prepared her for this.

Behind them, the Olympic Mountains were etched against the pink-and-orange sky. The Cascades towered even higher in front of them, their snow-white tops shining in the last of the sunlight. To the South, the impossible volcanic mass of Mount Rainier soared.

Seattle danced like fairy lights across the dark expanse of Puget Sound.

No, she had no idea what "that" was about, but she had to get away from Cassidy's home—it was the absolute strangest place she'd ever been.

The house was small without being cramped. Quiet. Quieter than the dorms and *way* quieter than New Jersey. It was nestled in the middle of a grape vineyard with no one near. No one to call for help. No one to ignore those cries either. It was so neat and tidy—too neat and tidy. The only thing out of place were the stacks of books that seemed to be mounded everywhere.

And Cassidy's father... Perrin shuddered. She didn't know what to make of Vic Knowles.

When he'd hugged Cassidy as they walked in, Perrin had been ready to gouge his eyes out with her nails—even if they were chewed short. But all he'd done was hug his daughter, kiss her on top of the head, and tell her how much he'd missed her. He'd then shaken Jo's hand. Perrin hadn't let him touch her, instead keeping her hands jammed in her pockets.

Rather than grabbing at her, he'd wished her welcome.

Like he was in some movie or something.

"What's that?" Perrin pointed at the colored lights that appeared to be floating in front of the city.

"The Christmas boat parade. It's a local tradition. Owners decorate their boats with Christmas lights and go from harbor to harbor for the two weeks before Christmas. Listen, you can just hear the Christmas carols."

The lead tour boat had a band out on the deck and sure enough, they were rocking out to Christmas.

"Let's go!"

"The lead boat costs money to go on. The others are private and you have to know someone."

Perrin leaned out against the rail. "Still, it's so dreamy, Cassidy. Someday can't you just picture us doing that. You'll marry someone alarmingly rich and handsome. He'll take you sailing on a huge sailboat, then Jo and I can come along for the ride and meet his amazingly successful friends."

Cassidy's sudden laugh said that wasn't very likely. Which was true. They were three of the poorest kids on campus, and everyone knew it. The cattier girls wouldn't let them forget it either—though she managed to deflect most of that away from Jo and Cassidy by making herself the target. She didn't care what any of them thought about her. As far as she was concerned, there were her two friends—and then there was everybody else. Nothing the others did mattered even a little in that world.

And here, on the ferry in the growing darkness, they were amazingly free of it all.

"Feel the wind!" Perrin spread her arms as if she could capture it and fly away.

"It's cold," Cassidy huddled at the rail, pulling her coat tighter. Jo didn't react at all, probably her Alaskan blood.

"No wind in space." That was her fantasy place of safety. They couldn't touch her in space. If only she could *be* one of those *Star Trek* women. Any of them. The good men in space didn't strike, beat, take—except a few villains who always died by the end of the episode.

"It's probably colder in space but that's hard to imagine at the moment." Cassidy muttered. But Perrin knew it was warmer here than it had been at school in New York.

"Inside, you silly. Spaceships are always the right tempera-ture inside."

"Good idea." And Cassidy pushed back through the heavy steel doors into the crowded sitting area. Jo offered a friendly shrug before following silently behind her.

Perrin gripped the rail and stared out at the city. Cities she understood. After four months of pussyfooting around the rules at Vassar College, she was going to explode. But she'd kept it reeled in because she didn't dare blow her ride. She'd landed a full scholarship based on standardized tests—like it was so hard to get a 1600 on the SATs—and the total shit-fiction essay she'd written for the application about "her hopes of building a better future for humankind." It had been exactly what they wanted to hear in their pretty little ivy-covered halls.

All she cared about was that the Pine Barrens stayed right the fuck in southern New Jersey and that she never again went near it. If the gods loved her, the swamp would suck down her parents even if it would turn it into a toxic waste dump when that happened. But the gods had proved they didn't exist years ago.

Her breathing slowly returned to normal as she gulped down the sea air.

She was in the middle of the water and she was alone. The water. Thirty feet to the night-black water. No, killing herself wasn't the answer either. That had been a much harder choice...before.

And thank God she hadn't because now she had a best friend. She couldn't do that to Cassidy. It might kill *her*. She liked Jo. Liked her steadiness, even trusted her. But she wasn't Cassidy. She wasn't—

"Enjoying the wind?" A deep voice asked from close beside her.

—alone.

He was a big guy. They were the only two out on the foredeck. Everyone else slouched in their soft seats behind the ferry's thick glass windows. He looked rough with a two-day beard and too-long hair that matched his leather motorcycle jacket and jeans. His eyes looked equally dark in the evening light. She'd gone for his type a lot. Dangerous. Hoping one would kill her parents for her.

None had.

All her mother had ever asked was how much she was charging the johns per hour, because Mom always got her cut, though Perrin never had when Mom sold her. Dear Mom had even done several of Perrin's partners herself for free just as a power play. After Perrin had burned their motorcycles, word got around and they steered clear of the crazy girl.

"Me and Santa. The wind makes us both fly. I'm gonna fly onto his lap tonight and make me a wish," she told Mr. Dark and Dangerous beneath the darkening sky.

He made a show of scanning her up and down. Her winter coat was knee-length, thrift-store wool. The wind pressed the soft-worn material tight against her.

"Not sure I like him getting all the fun."

"Oh, he won't." She didn't even know what she was saying. It didn't matter. This was just some ritual dance. And with the timing right, she turned and strode inside. He followed her only with his gaze, but she could feel its heat even after she found the other two and sat with her back to the foredeck. It was *all* about *who* controlled the dance.

# CHAPTER 3

*T*he two biggest cities Jo had ever been in were Juneau, Alaska, and New York. But neither one counted really. The first had been to catch the airplane east and the second had been to switch from the plane to the train up to Vassar. All she'd seen of New York had been underground, inside a subway car.

Seattle was a bewildering wonderland.

The ferry had landed them at the foot of downtown and Cassidy had led the way up steep, icy sidewalks into the heart of the city. There were Christmas lights and people everywhere. The clouds of their breath gave the colored lights halos and sparkles.

Each clothing window they passed, Perrin made a show of posing in front of each mannequin and asking, "How would this look on me?"

It didn't matter if it was an evening gown or a man's suit, they would all look good on Perrin's slender frame, though her candy-cane-striped hair clashed badly—or should have. On Perrin it was just cute and funny.

Perrin managed to nudge Cassidy in front of a window of wedding dresses.

"Nope, none of those would suit you. Not good enough," was Perrin's verdict in front of each dress.

Perrin had declared Cassidy as the "middle child" of the three of them. She had a nice figure and soft brunette hair down to her shoulders that matched her kind eyes.

Jo refused when Perrin tried to get her to stand in front of a wild flamenco gown. Her own big curves and dusky skin had come from her Tlingit ancestry, not Spain. She glanced at her reflection in the window, something she did only rarely. Her straight black hair that fell to the middle of her back was Native Alaskan as well. Only her face didn't fit. But there was no photo of her mother who'd left when she was two. Perhaps Jo's face was her mother's, but she hoped not. She didn't want anything from the woman who had broken her father—never a strong man to begin with.

"Spoilsport! I'll get you in a flamenco-style dress one of these days and you'll look a-ma-zing." Then Perrin had spotted an ad photo on a bus stop rain shelter and pushed Jo up against it before Jo could stop her. "Nope! Never mind. You're prettier than that. C'mon." And she led off as if this was her city and not Cassidy's.

Jo stepped away and turned to look at the image. It was one of the top supermodels ever, Naomi Campbell, modeling a mostly non-existent swimsuit in the middle of winter, "For that Getaway Vacation."

"She's nuts," Jo whispered to Cassidy.

"Heard that!" Perrin called out from impossibly too far away to hear. She circled back. "Not really. What did you say? Something scathing? Did our ever-proper Jo insult me behind my back? Was it crass? Was it *crude?*"

"What's with you and clothes? And your hair?" She didn't

think there was any set of circumstances under which calling Perrin nuts would turn out well.

"Don't you ever want to be someone other than you?"

Jo glanced at Cassidy who offered an infinitesimal shake of her head.

"I've worked my whole life to make me *who* I am. Why would I want to change that?" Jo couldn't imagine it.

In third grade, her best friend's dad had died on a crab boat. With that thin thread cut, the family moved back in with the grandparents in Anchorage, taking away Jo's only real friend in school. That was the day she'd sworn that she wouldn't end up a Ketchikan fisherman's wife and she had not veered once since. She was going to change her life—permanently.

Jo had found her way out: hard work and hard study until she was old enough to paste together a dozen different native, legal, and Alaskan scholarships. She'd only applied to East Coast schools; Vassar had been the one willing to make up the out-of-state difference. It didn't hurt that she factored into their new diversity initiative: Native Americans on campus—one.

Perrin shook her head. "I'm eighteen! I've spent my whole life waiting to escape and become someone new. Let's go!"

And she charged ahead once more.

The only way they kept from losing her in the crowd was by linking arms, Cassidy to one side and herself to the other. It slowed Perrin down enough for Jo to see some of the city, but not much.

Trees were wrapped in twinkle lights. Bright "Happy Holiday" banners fluttered in the breeze from lampposts. Cassidy led them to a park in the middle of the city that had scads of shoppers, even more decorated trees, and a small carousel. Perrin dragged them aboard for a ride even though the next oldest on the ride was about six.

She made everything more alive, more fun.

Jo felt Perrin tugging at something elusive. Some part of her that fit like it was her skin, but it wasn't. When she was with Perrin, Jo could feel...the possibility of the world. As if Seattle was rife with opportunity.

She began looking more at the city and less at the decorations and street-corner Santas. They were going to be just a half-hour ferry ride from this city for the next three weeks. Now that she was in college, it was time to start looking at what came next.

Jo inspected Perrin in some surprise as she realized what her friend was stripping away.

She was, in her crazed fashion, stripping away the heavy cloak of Jo's past.

Her analytical self wanted to ask how. Her rational self knew that Perrin would have no idea, but she was doing it anyway.

It was going to be a very interesting Christmas.

# CHAPTER 4

"This is all...wrong." Cassidy wished she'd never come.

For a gazillion years seeing "Santa at the Bon Marché" had been a rite of passage for Seattle children. Now, courtesy of a corporate buyout, it was a Macy's store. Which was only the first problem.

The second was that they were three grown women surrounded by little boys and girls in that ecstatic state of sugar-induced near-coma. Hadn't the three of them just been browsing the racks looking at dresses they could never afford? Grown-up dresses.

Perrin had led them into the high-end racks. There she'd forced her to try on a dark jade-green velvet dress that had looked incredible in the mirror. Which it should as it cost more than a month's college tuition, including room and board.

"You should totally steal that dress, Cassidy," Perrin had called out loudly enough to get the department clerk's undivided attention. By the time she'd changed out of it, one of the store detectives was standing quietly at the far end of the department but keeping a close eye on them.

Even back on the hanger Cassidy couldn't stop touching it.

Perrin slipped a hand around her waist. "You really did look incredible in that. I wish I could just buy it for you and then you could break hearts all over campus."

"Thanks, Perrin." Cassidy leaned into her for a quiet moment before Perrin had flitted off finding the *perfect* hat for Jo—which so looked like it was meant for a tasteless trip to the Bahamas that they were all laughing together a moment later.

Now she was in line with little kids among Christmas elves her own age. The elves, dressed in brilliant green-and-red felt suits, rolled their eyes at them.

Cassidy did her best to look invisible while Perrin tried to finagle an elf costume for herself with no success.

Without her really noticing, Jo had drifted out of the line. She blended in so well that it took some effort for Cassidy to spot her. Jo appeared to be making a careful inspection of a toy display as if she was just another waiting parent seeking patience.

Cassidy had no idea how she'd done it. Every time she tried to follow Jo, Perrin would hyper up or snag her arm and ask some ridiculous question that Cassidy couldn't resist answering.

Without any warning, it was their turn.

Before Santa managed so much as a, "Ho! Ho! Ho!" Perrin was planted on Santa's lap.

"Looking for a Mrs. Claus for the night?" She wrapped her arms around his neck and planted a big sloppy kiss on his cheek.

"Uh, no. Mrs. Claus is waiting at home for this Santa."

"How sad for me. There goes my wish of having a Santa for Christmas. So what does Santa wish for Christmas if it isn't two beautiful, nubile women?" Perrin winked broadly at Cassidy.

Cassidy could feel the heat soaring to her cheeks.

"How about something more practical?" He held out a lollipop from a stash he clearly kept for troublesome children.

"Deal! Works for me, Santa," Perrin kissed his cheek just like a little girl and jumped off his lap. "But Cassidy is special. She'll need something much more amazing than this," she unwrapped her lollipop and stuffed it in her mouth. "Oh, grape! You're an awesome Santa. Your turn, Cassidy. Sit! Sit! Sit!"

Unable to escape Perrin's jubilant insistence, Cassidy eased down gently on Santa's knee.

"Ho! Ho! Ho! And Merry Christmas. Has Cassidy been a good girl this year?"

"I've...tried."

"Better than awesome," Perrin chimed in, "like uber-awesome-sauce."

"Well, that's good news. Santa likes putting better-than-awesome girls at the top of his list. What does Cassidy want for Christmas?"

At Perrin's insistence, Cassidy had put on her best clothes, carefully selected from the Goodwill rack. She knew she stood out horribly from all of the pretty moms with their warmly dressed children. She also knew how hard her father worked for every bottle of wine so she never spent a penny she didn't have to.

"But..."

"But what, Cassidy?" Santa asked in such a kind voice that she couldn't help answering.

"A nice dress. I'd like a really nice dress. One to make the boys at the college dances notice me." She'd felt beautiful for that single moment in front of the mirror wearing that lovely and terribly impractical dress.

Every boy noticed Perrin.

And Jo had carefully selected a fellow pre-law student as quiet and understated as she was. She'd hinted that she might date him for all four years simply to avoid unwanted distractions.

Cassidy was lost somewhere in the middle.

Santa patted her gently on the back. "You *are* a good girl. You just keep being yourself, Cassidy, and Santa will see what he can do."

As she pushed to her feet he held out a lemon lollipop and she squeezed his hand in thanks as she took it.

Perrin was unusually quiet as they exited between the plastic reindeer and another pair of college-aged elves. They turn to track down Jo in the crowded store.

"What?" It was such an unusual state that Cassidy stopped Perrin once they were out of the way.

"How did you end up being...you?" This wasn't the manic Perrin, nor the sad one. This one was new, quiet and thoughtful.

"I don't know. Dad says I've always been like this, even before Mom died. He calls me Ice Sweet. Icewine is rare and very sweet. The grapes are left to dry and freeze on the vine then they're harvested around my birthday, December twenty-first. You can't really do it here because the winter isn't consistently cold enough. I try to remain cool like the wine but sweet too. I guess. That's kinda all muddled up, but that's how I always thought of it as a kid."

"Your dad...cares about you."

"And me about him. He's the best."

Perrin remained quiet until they tracked down Jo. She was in a deep discussion with a small boy about the advantages and disadvantages of a toy airplane versus a very red firetruck.

At the archway leading out of Santa's domain they passed a man completely out of place. A biker guy slouched against a column. His smile had mothers herding their children ahead as they scurried by.

"We need a bar!" Wild Perrin was back. "A good Seattle dive bar. Captain Janeway wants a Christmas par-*tay!*"

# CHAPTER 5

"They're not very good," Jo shouted over the band, but Perrin didn't care.

Most of the people at the Central Saloon in Pioneer Square didn't care. When three pretty girls showed up in a row, they hadn't even cared to check their IDs. She had snuck Cassidy and Jo into a couple of New York bars before, so they hadn't protested too much.

Between its narrow brick walls was a massive bar, a scattering of tables, and a large open area for dancing. The retro band was rocking out bad covers of Bon Jovi, The B-52's, and Blondie. At this rate, they'd be playing ABBA and the Stones next, not that she cared about that either as long as she could drink and dance.

She leaned with her back against the bar between Cassidy and Jo when the bartender tapped her on the shoulder. He waved to a drink he'd just set down. It was in a V-shaped martini glass, filled with bright pink.

"What is it?"

"A Cosmo, Cosmopolitan. Guy said a woman like you shouldn't be drinking beer."

"Which guy?" She had to shout over a blast of sound that might be AC/DC's "Highway to Hell" if it was done by Maroon 5 on drugs. At least the last part was probably accurate.

The bartender shrugged and moved off.

Perrin knocked back a mouthful. Cranberries plus a hard kick of alcohol and enough lime juice punch to smooth it out.

"Where did you get that?" Cassidy shouted.

"Some guy."

"Hey! You can't drink that. You don't know what they did to it," Cassidy grabbed for it, so Perrin knocked it back quick.

"Get a life, Cass. I'm here with you, how much trouble can I get into?"

"That's what worries me."

Perrin barely heard her as she scanned the crowd. Drink buyers were typically easy to pick out, though less so tonight. The three of them lined up at the bar were drawing a lot of looks from the guys.

Wait, the drink had come from the bartender, which meant someone along the bar.

Ooo! Mr. Dark and Dangerous had followed her from Santa's and the ferry was looking her way. Maybe she'd get her Christmas wish after all.

She moved onto the dance floor, keeping her back to the bar, just dancing in the crowd to what had turned out to be Foreigner's "Cold as Ice." When his hand slid around her waist from behind, she didn't turn, but found the rhythm of her body against his.

Oh yeah, she knew how to, she sang along with the refrain, *sacrifice her love.*

# CHAPTER 6

"*Where* did she go?"

The pressure from the crowded bar had Jo closing the gap with Cassidy. They'd only looked away from the dance floor long enough to decide if they could afford to split another beer.

But when Jo looked back, there was no sign of Perrin.

Cassidy turned to scan the crowd as well.

Perrin's candy-cane hair should have been easy to spot.

Jo felt like they were secret agents as Cassidy flashed a couple hand signs over the roar of Phil Collin's "Sussudio" or something very like it.

Without a word, they circled the perimeter of the room in opposite directions.

Jo didn't find anyone in the women's bathroom. And thankfully a guy exiting the men's just as she arrived at the door, told her it was empty.

Under the band's high platform was all dark shadows, but no sign of Perrin or the man she'd been dancing with.

She met Cassidy, pinned against the brick wall by the press of dancers, on the side of the hall opposite the bar. Jo noted that despite not have candy-striped hair they'd found each other easily. Perrin definitely wasn't here.

Cassidy pointed to the front door in question.

Jo sighed. It seemed the only likely answer.

Together they headed out into the cold.

Despite the rare freezing temperatures, the streets of Pioneer Square were lively with tourists gawking just as obviously as she'd been. Then she heard it. A rare sound to her ear, a couple of police cars racing toward them with their sirens going.

In Ketchikan, the police were mainly involved with breaking up bar fights, taking home drunks, and delivering the bad news to families when a boat was lost at sea.

Here, in a huge city like Seattle, it seemed to Jo that there were sirens every time she turned around.

# CHAPTER 7

*C*assidy wouldn't have really noticed the sirens if Jo hadn't pointed them out. Seattle had them now and then. She'd spent several days staying in a youth hostel and exploring New York before taking the train up to college. The sirens had been so constant that Seattle sounded strangely quiet in comparison. But when two police cars raced toward them from opposite directions along First Avenue then both turned sharply onto Yesler Way, she felt a chill that had nothing to do with the cold.

"Please keep going."

Her prayer wasn't answered.

She heard the screech of tires from around the corner and could see the whirling police car lights flashing off the buildings.

She led Jo up the short side street to Occidental Avenue at a sprint.

The two cars had slammed to a stop at the other end of the block and the officers were climbing out of their cars. Their weapons weren't drawn, but they had their hands on them as they walked into the Saveway Market. It was a corner convenience store that catered mostly to the homeless in the area. The sort of place where they sold pre-peeled hard-boiled eggs from a jar of water, and offered use of a can opener with the sale of SpaghettiOs and included a plastic spoon without asking.

Cassidy edged along the block until she could see into the window between the rusted iron bars and the curling beer signs plastering the inside of the glass.

One of the policeman was standing back while the other went up to the counter. By the old clerk's gestures, he was describing an event, but Cassidy didn't see anyone.

"I have a very bad feeling about this," Jo whispered over her shoulder.

"Me too. But maybe she got away?" Cassidy knew that the chances of that working for long were slim. No one stood out in a crowd like Perrin.

"She could be anywhere."

She could be, but Cassidy wondered. If things had gone wrong and chaotic Perrin crashed into sad Perrin... "Come on."

It really wasn't in her to cross between the store and the police cars, but she didn't feel as if she had any choice. She tried to be casual as she glanced into the store at what was happening, but her knees were shaking so badly that she almost stumbled into the door jamb like a wandering drunk.

She made the corner.

Straight ahead was one of the strangest parking garages ever built. It was a steeply sloped two-level garage that had been built on a triangular patch left over by the junction of three main streets. She'd always imagined it was the prow of a sinking ship which was far too apt a metaphor at the moment.

"You think she's in there?"

Cassidy didn't know what to think, but she didn't want the police to think it strange they were hanging out on the corner.

She turned left, toward the heart of Pioneer Square once more, when she saw a tall man in a black motorcycle jacket stride out the end of the narrow alley between Occidental and First. He glanced their way, the flashing police cars lights lit the avaricious smile on his face, then he turned left and strolled away into the evening crowd.

He looked vaguely familiar, and that worried her. She'd seen him somewhere.

"Santa," Jo gasped out.

"He wasn't Santa. But I think that's the guy she was just dancing with."

"No, yes, I mean..."

It was one of the few times Cassidy had ever heard Jo be flustered.

"Yes, he's the guy she danced with. But he was there at Santa's, watching us when we left. He made me think of the kind of person that restraining orders were made for. I was reading about those in my criminal law book."

Together they hurried to the mouth of the alley. It was narrow, dark, and smelly. There were Dumpsters behind each business, though she couldn't imagine how a garbage truck fit down the lane.

Jo reached into her purse. "I have some Mace." She held up a small can.

Taking bravery from her practical roommate that she didn't have herself, they crept down the alley.

They didn't have to go far. Even in the dim light, Cassidy recognized Perrin's coat around the figure crumpled against the wall.

"Are you okay?" Cassidy knelt beside her.

"My head hurts." Perrin's voice was a little hazy.

Cassidy pulled off the black wool hat that covered Perrin's hair and began probing around.

"Ow! Hey!"

Cassidy checked her fingers. "Big lump. No blood."

"He just slammed me against the wall. Shit! What's with the cop lights?"

Cassidy glanced at Jo. In seconds, they had Perrin on her feet and were stumbling together the other way down the long dark alley.

# CHAPTER 8

*P*errin had nodded her head 'yes' until the pain became too much as Cassidy had lectured her last night all the way back to the ferry. As its engines started, adding to her pounding headache, Cassidy's voice had become shrill.

*Do you* want *to die?*

She'd finally told Cassidy the truth to shut her up, that she'd never expected to live to eighteen in the first place. All that had done was make her best friend incredibly sad. *Real smooth, Perrin.*

Then Cassidy had overcompensated by setting an alarm to wake Perrin every hour to make sure she hadn't slipped into a concussion coma.

As to the punch and the sore head, neither was new territory. It didn't really matter anyway, the old guy only had a hundred bucks in the till. That Mr. Nameless had taken her half-share sucked, but it wasn't even close to what she would've needed to buy Cassidy that dress for Christmas.

Staring into the bathroom mirror this morning at her purpling jaw, Perrin pulled out a tube of coverup. Dabbing and blending until everything looked clear—except her eyes. She had no way to cover up her eyes so that she didn't have to see herself in them.

"Think, Perrin, think! You're an idiot. Cass knows you're broke. You magically buy her that dress and she's gonna know you stole the money." The clarity of daylight sucked.

Then she spotted Jo in the mirror.

"Hey! Bathroom. Private."

"It is if you actually lock the door or answer when I knock." Jo stepped in and made a show of closing and locking it. Then she moved up close enough that they were both looking in the same small mirror. Jo didn't usually get so close.

"What? Didn't I cover it well enough?" Perrin checked her chin in the mirror again.

"You look fine, Perrin. You really did all that to buy a dress for Cassidy?"

"I really need to learn to keep my voice down when I'm talking to myself."

Whereas Jo used her silence like a weapon, some kind of creepy lawyer thing. Perrin tried to wait her out...but couldn't.

"Don't you ever even blink? You're gonna scare the shit out of juries someday." Perrin sat on the closed toilet and looked up at Jo. "It was Cassidy's wish to Santa last night. She wanted that dress I forced her into. I just wanted to do something nice for her."

"So earn the money."

Perrin laughed. "How?"

"A lot of those stores we passed last night were advertising for Christmas clerk help."

"They were? I could be...an elf?"

Jo offered one of those quiet smiles that must be an Alaska laugh. "I've encountered worse ideas."

"And what are you going to do?"

Jo picked up a brush, turned back to the mirror, and began brushing out her hair. "That's an interesting question."

"To which, counselor, the answer might be?" Perrin did her best to sound like Judge Judy.

"As I stated, it *is* an interesting question. I liked Seattle—"

"Until I fucked it up."

"—until you fucked it up." Jo nodded. "Something you said made me wonder…"

But no matter how Perrin pried, she didn't get any more out of Jo.

Not even when they took the ferry back into Seattle after breakfast—without Cassidy.

# CHAPTER 9

Jo started at the Seattle Public Library. They directed her to the Puget Sound Business Journal's annual summary of law firms. This was a far safer place to make rookie mistakes, well away from the New York law firms she eventually hoped to impress.

Starting at the top of the list, she called each human resources department and asked for an informational interview. Out of the top ten firms, she managed to set one interview for that afternoon and two for the next morning. After visiting a stationery store to acquire a small leather notebook and a cheap, but professional-looking pen, she spent the rest of the day drafting up her list of questions.

After the first was over, Jo suspected that she'd learned too much at her very first interview. The next two confirmed her initial assessment.

If her desire was to become a cog in a massive corporate machine, struggling for years to climb from the morass of new-associate obscurity, then she would choose a large law firm.

A mid-sized firm agreed to see her in two more days. They offered a somewhat better chance: fifty attorneys, seventeen of them partners, and only five new associates each year. It would be far easier to shine in a smaller pond—until she'd asked her last question.

"After seven years on the associate track, when was the last associate offered a partnership?"

One man, three years before.

The other associates could stay as worker bees but would never make the partnership grade. Or they'd be gone to other firms, starting on another seven-year climb of chance.

By Cassidy's birthday party on the winter solstice, Jo was little wiser about how to best launch a career after law school.

# CHAPTER 10

"*A*re you doing okay, Daddy?"

"What? Who? Me? Fine. I'm doing fine, Ice Sweet."
Vic Knowles tried to retreat back into his book, but Cassidy
could see that he knew he wasn't fooling either of them, so he
closed it without even remembering to put in a bookmark. "It's
just mid-winter. Nothing worse than a vintner in mid-winter.
No harvest, no pruning until March. Other than tending the
young wine every now and then, it gets awfully quiet."

Cassidy sat in her habitual overstuffed chair, just a side table
away from her father's worn armchair. *Been sitting in it since
before you were born, girl. I'll be dying right in this same chair
someday if I'm lucky.* They shared a smile over his habitual
phrase without either of them saying it aloud.

"I'm sorry that I'm so far away." She still remembered his
pained expression when she'd told him she'd chosen Vassar.

"It's right where you're supposed to be, Cassidy. Your mom
would have loved that you're there in the same school she
went to."

Yet Cassidy wasn't so sure. It seemed like there was
supposed to be something more. Someday the winery would be

hers...if she wanted it. She wasn't even sure about that. But she absolutely knew that she never wanted to disappoint her father either. Vassar wasn't teaching what she needed to know.

"The marketing and economics courses are good there," Daddy placed his vote.

"You've been reading my course catalogs again."

He smiled a little and reached over the other side of his chair. Then he lifted up a battered used copy of her first semester textbook. "I've got a question."

She couldn't help but laugh. So many nights the two of them had spent the evenings working their way through her homework together. Cassidy had quickly learned to do the math and science while he was still out tending the vines, but they could stay up to midnight talking about a single poem together.

The marketing book, as they delved into it, let her sketch down some ideas for Daddy to use here at the winery. It made her feel less far away, closer to home. Not quite "where she belonged" anymore, but still definitely home.

"I do worry about your friends, Ice Sweet."

That stopped her in the middle of trying to explain the reasons to invest in a website. "It's not the 1990s anymore, Daddy. We're in the Os or the Aughts or whatever. People actually use the Internet to look things up now. You could get a head start on so many others."

He had nodded his head in that way that said it wasn't going to happen. Maybe she'd do it herself from New York. She could get some lessons over at the school's tech center. But that wasn't her concern at the moment.

"My friends?"

"I like Jo. She's not exactly warm, but I like her. And she's incredibly smart. I like that your roommate is someone smart."

Jo was brilliant enough that Cassidy was a little glad that they didn't overlap on any classes.

But that meant he didn't like Perrin.

"Why not?"

"She's…" Daddy shrugged, "a little wild for my taste."

"Says the man who grew up in the '60s."

"In a rural farming town and then went to Vietnam in the early '70s," his voice went grim as it always did and she was sorry she'd said anything. But she also know how to get him out of it.

"Then there was Mom." And a smile broke out on his face as he sighed more easily. Cassidy had always known what true love was, even though she'd only ever seen half of it. It was the look on her father's face every time he thought of Mom.

"There was. I used to call her the Last of the Hippies. I still can't believe that she chose to grow grapes with me rather than going to grad school. I think it's the only fight we ever had, and she won, of course. All these years and I still don't get it."

Cassidy totally did, Vic Knowles was the best "guy" in the world. His winery wasn't a big success, but it wasn't a failure by a long way. He was the best father she could imagine—especially when she heard stories from Jo and considered whatever darkness Perrin went to when talk turned to families.

"No," he held up a hand to stop her going down that track, "you're my daughter which makes you totally biased on my behalf."

"It doesn't mean I'm wrong about Perrin."

Daddy just grimaced.

"Perrin is…" Cassidy didn't know how to explain her friend. After that horrible night in Pioneer Square, she'd kept an unusually low profile. So had Jo, now that she thought about it. They were always back in the evening but were both gone during the day. She'd been so happy to be home, she hadn't thought much of it. But…

She shook her head to clear it.

"Perrin is—"

"Ready for a par-*tay!*" Perrin raced into the living room at her normal manic speed and tossed her coat and hat over a pile of books. *"Happy birthday to you, oh-Cassidy-the-awesome. Happy birthd—"*

"Hey. I asked you to wait for me," Jo came in to stand beside Perrin. Her coat would, of course, be hung up in the hallway above her wet boots.

"You only asked. I never said yes." Perrin did restart the song thought so that Jo and Daddy could join in.

Cassidy did her best to look grateful but could feel the heat come to her cheeks for being the center of attention.

"Blow out the candles!" Perrin shouted.

"There isn't any cake."

"Yet," Daddy pointed toward the kitchen. "After dinner."

"No, first!" Perrin collapsed in a heap on the sofa. "'Life is uncertain. Eat dessert first.' Ernestine Ulmer 1925. Though I prefer Helen Keller's 'Life is short and unpredictable. Eat the dessert first.' Such an amazing woman. She's my idol."

"You'd never survive," Jo said drily.

"Being deaf and blind?" Perrin cocked her head as if really thinking about it. "Yeah, it's a tough road, but I bet I could pull it off."

Cassidy couldn't stop her laugh.

"What?" Perrin put on her best 'hurt' look.

"You, not having a whirlwind of people around you who you can bounce off of all at once."

"Yeah," Perrin slouched lower and crossed her feet on top of a stack of books beside the coffee table which instantly scattered across the rug. Her feet remained crossed in mid-air over what was now empty space. "That would suck."

# CHAPTER 11

*C*assidy's laugh as she batted at Perrin's airborne feet was the best. So Perrin held them up in the air until her gut muscles were screaming just to tease the birthday girl.

Of course she might as well be deaf and blind at the moment for all the good it was doing her. Dumb too for that matter. No one in all of Seattle had been willing to take a chance on the girl with the candy-stripe hair and a shabby winter coat stained by whatever nastiness she'd collapsed into in that alley.

No one except a family Mexican restaurant over in Bell-town, a few blocks north of Pike Place Market. Cash, under the table, if she'd clear tables and wash dishes. The Mamá had made it clear that if some inspector came in, she was doing it for free as research for some school project. She was forbidden from touching food unless it was served to her on a plate at lunchtime, like she would have had any clue about Mexican food or anything else her mom hadn't served out of a can.

There was sure no English spoken in the kitchen and she didn't speak Spanish. So she could hear but it didn't matter. And in the back, no one except for the teen boy spoke English, but he was too tongue-tied around her to reply even when she spoke directly to him.

And blind. She could wish she was blind. People were such slobs when they ate. Everything she cleaned up reminded her only too well of the trailer trash she'd grown up with.

"You okay?" Cassidy had settled on the couch beside her without Perrin noticing.

"Who? Me? I'm Perrin, I'm always fine!"

Cassidy exchanged some look with her father. But Perrin still didn't know how to interpret his expressions. She'd come to think that maybe, just maybe, he was okay. Yet more than one professor at school had made it clear that she had an alternate path to an easy A—as if.

There actually had been job offers in Pike Place Market, but the few she found all came with the price she was less and less willing to pay.

Perrin didn't like getting caught, even by Cassidy, so she kept her "happy" self out front all through dinner until it was time for the cake.

"Presents!" Perrin shouted and raced back to her coat that she had draped over Cassidy's present so as not to tear the thin paper.

She'd wrapped it in a page of the Sunday comics from *The Seattle Times,* so at least it was fun and colorful.

But maybe it was too stupid, so despite her rush to fetch it, she nudged Jo to go first.

Jo's gift was so small that Perrin felt better, until Cassidy opened it.

"It's a really good pen. I found this tiny pen store in the Market. It's a little scuffed up, so they sold it to me at, um, a price I could afford."

Cassidy and her dad made a thing about the pen like it was something special. Perrin wrote and sometimes drew with the ten-pack of colored ballpoints for two dollars.

Her dad reached under his chair and pulled out his gift. Gifts. One was big and heavy the other small.

Now Perrin felt awful. She wished she'd gone first so that it wasn't such a let-down at the end.

The small one was a pocket-sized wine journal in tool-worked leather. Each page was pre-printed with ratings for aspects of wine that she'd never even heard of: body, balance, and finish. There was a "flavor wheel" for marking words like: tannic, spicy, grassy, and all sorts of odd things. The second was the little journal's big brother with room for pasting in labels and photographs and writing whole paragraphs about the stuff.

"Oh, Daddy," Cassidy hugged them to her chest like she'd been given the moon. She leaned into him without hesitation and he hugged her tightly.

Perrin watched closely but it was just a hug.

"You have *such* an amazing palate, Ice Sweet. And you're in New York which I've read has a whole set of its own amazing wines. You can record each one and then tell me about them whenever you come home. Then I can pretend I've been there. Maybe even bring a bottle of your favorite one for us to taste together."

Cassidy just sniffled and nodded against his shoulder as she still clutched the books to her chest.

Perrin looked down at her ill-wrapped lump of a gift.

No!

It was too stupid to give to Cassidy.

Perrin pushed back from the table and raced up the narrow stairway. They were all three camped in Cassidy's small room, so no privacy there.

She locked herself in the bathroom, climbed into the tub, and pulled the curtain, clutching the stupid present in its stupid paper to her stupid flat chest.

There was a knock on the door.

"Go away!"

There was a small click and the door unlocked. Cassidy pushed the door open and then hung a fat paperclip on some hook outside.

Perrin watched her through the gap in the shower curtain.

"I locked myself in by accident once when I was little. I was kinda freaked by the time Dad found me, too young to understand door locks. I screamed when he left me to get the paperclip. He had me help him hang it outside the door so he wouldn't have to leave to unlock it if it ever happened again. It didn't, of course."

Cassidy stepped in, closed the door, and sat on the edge of the tub. She didn't ask anything, she just sat and waited.

Perrin pulled up her knees and rested her forehead on them, but Cassidy didn't go away.

"Here!" She dragged out the stupid present, half tearing the newsprint, and held it out without looking up.

She could hear Cassidy opening it carefully, undoing each bit of tape. "Christ, Cassidy, it's just the funnies page."

Still she didn't tear it.

Perrin waited for the laugh. But Cassidy was too nice for that and would now say something fake. Except Cassidy never did that either.

Finally Perrin looked up.

Cassidy was rubbing it against her cheek and spoke with a sense of wonder, "It's so soft."

"It's cashmere. I wanted to get you that dress, but I couldn't figure out how to steal it, so I stole you this instead."

Cassidy dropped it as if it burned her fingers. "Stole it? We have to take it back right away. How could you—"

"Jesus, Cassidy, you really *are* you, aren't you? I knew you'd be like that. No, I didn't steal it. I bought it."

Cassidy didn't look convinced, though her hand reached out to stroke it again.

"I've got the receipt. Somewhere...I think...unless I lost it. But I did pay for it."

"How?"

Perrin couldn't stand that look on Cassidy's face. "With money I earned. For the last four days I've been washing dishes in a hole-in-the-wall restaurant so I could buy that for you. Okay? Happy?"

Cassidy didn't look at the scarf. Instead she held it up to her chest just like she had the wine journals from her father. But Cassidy looked her square in the eye. And started to cry.

"Oh God, you really are a mush, aren't you?"

Cassidy just nodded.

"They called it tomato red, but I think it's closer to cardinal red, you know, a little browner and richer. It'll really capture your hair color in sunlight. It'll make your skin even healthier and glowier than you already look as if that was possible. There was a hot pink one that would look awesome on you, but I know about you and bright colors."

"It's beautiful," Cassidy sniffled out as she rubbed it against her cheek once more, getting it damp with her tears.

"Hey, what's going on in here?" Jo stepped into the bathroom, saw Cassidy was crying, and scowled at Perrin like it was all her fault. She was half tempted to close the curtain on the both of them.

"Look, they're good tears, right Cass?"

Cassidy nodded and started crying more.

Perrin sighed, pulled on Cassidy until she collapsed into the tub and landed in her lap. Just like her father had, Perrin hugged her close.

"Why is she crying?" Jo sat on the edge of the tub where Cassidy had just been.

"How am I supposed to know? All I did was wash dishes in a Mexican restaurant to buy her a stupid scarf. Fair and square. I didn't steal anything from anybody, Jo." Perrin crossed her heart as well as she could with Cassidy sort of collapsed on top of her.

Now Jo's eyes were watering up. Then she did the craziest thing, undemonstrative Jo Thompson leaned over and kissed her soundly on top of the head.

"You did good, Perrin."

"Aw crap!" Now Perrin was the one getting the sniffles.

# CHAPTER 12

*J*o shouldn't have told anybody anything, but it had been a confessional sort of moment in the bathroom. After Cassidy's father had called them all back downstairs for cupcakes and candles, the conversation had started up again as they lay in Cassidy's room on foam pads.

She told about her "testing" the various types of law firms—and how disappointing they were being. How could she possibly practice law if she couldn't find a place in which she *wanted* to practice it?

That morning, before she'd left for her latest interview, Perrin had dragged out all of their clothes and made her change more times than a store mannequin.

All it had done was make her nerves escalate completely out of proportion to the likelihood of any positive outcome.

Now she stood in front of the smoked glass wall of the smallest firm she'd interviewed yet. Her reflection still surprised her. Perrin had insisted on strong colors rather than Jo's preferred beiges and creams. And much to her surprise, she had ended up in navy-blue slacks instead of a dress.

*You're taking on men on their home turf. You can't go in selling sex, they'll ignore you. You're already so beautiful that they can't ignore you, so don't go flaunting it.*

Jo took one last look at the reflected woman and wondered quite how Perrin had done it. She looked…successful.

"Look out, boys." Perrin had made her recite it so often as they came over on the ferry together that it seemed to hum inside Jo's head.

These weren't boys.

She was a first-year pre-law freshman at a small college three thousand miles away and they were an incredibly successful boutique law firm specializing in environmental law.

*Look out, boys.* Perrin's voice whispered inside her head. She stepped to the glass wall, which whooshed silently aside to let her into the inner sanctum. The lobby reeked of success and money.

Immediately the memory of the stench of her father's shack and his aging fishing boat made her like this firm—very much.

CHAPTER 13

*P*errin took the twenty thousandth load of garbage of *stank* out to the Dumpster behind the restaurant. At the same moment, the woman across the alley was carrying out a pillow-case-sized cloth bag filled with fabric. There were shots of cobalt blue, nimbus gray, and sunshine yellow peeking out the top.

She was lifting it into her own Dumpster when Perrin shouted to stop her.

"You're throwing all that out?"

"Sure." The woman was bone-thin, looked as if she'd been that way for her whole life.

"Why?"

"They're just scraps," she went to lift it again and Perrin hurried over to stop her. Then she realized she was still carrying the bulging sack of restaurant ick.

"Wait. Just wait." She turned back, threw out her own bag, did her best to wipe her hands on her soiled jeans, and hurried back over. "Can I see?"

The woman set the sack on the alley's brickwork.

Perrin peeked inside. Past the cobalt was saddle brown.

Under that four pieces of four different shades of lavender. "What's all this from?"

The woman dug into a pocket, pulled out a box of cigarettes, and tamped one free.

Perrin shook her head at the silent offer. Her mother smoked, so it was her one rule. She wouldn't even dance with a man who smoked, never mind screw him.

"I make clothes."

"You...*make* them?"

"You thought they grew on trees?"

"Only in Cinderella."

The woman barked out a laugh and followed it up with a hacking cough.

"You make your living making clothes?" Perrin dug her fingers deeper into the bag grabbed at random, and pulled up a piece of jade green satin almost the same color as the dress she'd wanted for Cassidy.

"Make enough to keep the flesh on my bones." She gave another smoker's laugh as she held up an arm that was bone, muscle, and skin without a single ounce of anything else.

"Can I keep this?"

"Diving before I even get it in the Dumpster? Welcome to it, girl." She scattered some ash off her cigarette with a wave and went inside, pulling the steel door shut behind her.

Perrin squatted over the bag, feeling the fabrics, letting their colors wash over her eyes and block out the brown and black of refried beans, the red of salsa, and the green of cilantro and jalapeño peppers.

Then she twisted to look to the west. Not at the restaurant. Or even Puget Sound. While she'd been poking around Cassidy's house she'd seen an old sewing machine covered in dust.

What if it still worked?

# CHAPTER 14

"**W**e can't!" Cassidy tried to pull back from the door.

"Oh yes we can! We're celebrating!" Perrin dragged her ahead.

"But we can't afford this," Jo was fighting back as well. Though they both easily outweighed her, together they were barely holding Perrin in check.

Perrin dug into her pocket and pulled out a wad of bills.

"Crap, Perrin. Did you knock over a bank?"

"No, a restaurant." Perrin rolled her eyes before Cassidy could speak. "Get a grip, Cassidy. I've slaved for two-and-a-half weeks for Mamá Estrada, she even gave me a bonus and told me about this place. We're heading back to college tomorrow, we should celebrate tonight."

"You should save that, Perrin."

"I already have…"

Cassidy made the mistake of relaxing her guard.

"For a moment just like this!" Perrin swept ahead, dragging them both through the doors before they could stop her.

Inside Cutter's Crabhouse they were greeted by a narrow hallway, one side lined by tropical fish tanks. Past those, the path split. To the right was a sign that said, Restaurant.

"Maybe we could get a table...and split an appetizer," Cassidy hedged, hoping that Jo would be okay with the inevitable.

Perrin swung them to the left into the bar.

It was brightly lit and classier than even the sort of places she and her father would go for a major celebration, like finishing a good harvest—a rare event in itself in the rainy Pacific Northwest. A quick glance at the plates set in front of the groups of beautiful people spoke of money. As did the people. The air also smelled of fine seasoning, fresh seafood, and, she sniffed again, at least one very nice wine.

"Here we go!" Manic Perrin raced across the bar to a recently vacated table, drawing every eye as always.

Except this time perhaps not for how pretty she was.

For the last two weeks, she'd spent every evening learning to use Cassidy's mother's vintage Singer sewing machine. Daddy had kept it for the memory and Cassidy had never learned to use it.

Perrin had. Her first clothes were odd; they were ill-fitting, bizarrely colored, and occasionally dissolved just by being tried on. But by making several dresses a night, she'd achieved some skill. Another bag of scraps had appeared from that dressmaker in Belltown, and Perrin had kept working.

Tonight she looked like a cross between a crazy-patch quilt and a sleek silver-and-orange space alien.

Which, impossibly, did look amazing on her.

She and Jo had managed to not have to wear any of Perrin's new creations tonight, though they'd certainly been test models for enough clothes these last weeks.

They reached the high-top table Perrin had captured just as

a waiter cleared away the remains of its prior occupants. It stood against the tall glass window that Cassidy had first thought was just filled with the night. Now she saw that the lights of the entire waterfront from Pike Place Market down to Pioneer Square was laid out below them. The dark waters of Puget Sound spread beyond, dotted with twinkling ferries crossing to Bremerton and Bainbridge Island which sparkled in the distance.

"I've having a Cosmo," Perrin informed the waiter. "These two are going to be boring, so bring them a bottle of some nice wine."

"Are you sure about the Cosmo?" Jo asked as she sat on the stool. "The last time didn't turn out so well."

Perrin grimaced, "I liked it. Besides, something good has to come from that night."

Cassidy gave up fighting and turned to the waiter, "An Oregon Pinot Gris, please. Nothing fancy."

The man nodded with perfect equanimity, "May I see your IDs?"

Cassidy froze. They were eighteen, not twenty-one. She hadn't been thinking.

Perrin didn't even hesitate as she handed over three New York State drivers licenses. The waiter inspected them, glanced around the table, and returned them without even a stray look before departing.

Cassidy snatched them from Perrin's hand.

Their photos were right off their student IDs, but all the rest of it looked very authentic, except they were all four years older and none of them were licensed to drive by New York.

"Perrin..." Cassidy waved them at her.

"Oh, come on. They were cheap. A guy on campus made them for me ages ago as a favor." Cassidy tried not to think about what price Perrin had probably paid, all too willingly.

The waiter returned with their drinks, turning the wine for Cassidy to inspect. She knew this wine, pleasant and not terribly expensive, though she wouldn't think about the restaurant markup. He had it uncorked before she had time to think they should have just had two glasses. Once again Perrin had somehow clouded their minds and gotten her way.

"To?" Perrin raised her bright pink Cosmo.

"No more stealing," Jo and Cassidy practically said in unison.

"Spoilsports," but Perrin raised her glass in acknowledgement and they toasted.

The waiter was unflappable as he laid out bar menus.

Perrin pointed to three things, apparently at random, then shooed the waiter away before Cassidy could stop him.

"We'll bloat."

"Nuh-uh. Okay, Rule Number One," Perrin raised her glass, "there's no such thing as calories or fat when the three of us are drinking together. So tonight we get to be as decadent as we want."

Cassidy glanced at Jo as the waiter delivered a slab of thick-sliced focaccia bread. It radiated warm rosemary-and-olive smells. Jo raised an eyebrow that said she'd heard of worse ideas.

They drank to Rule Number One, then Cassidy bit off a piece of the focaccia and decided that it was a fine rule.

"What are we celebrating again?"

Perrin struck a pose and floofed her candy-stripe hair. "My first dress that isn't a man-repellent *and* actually lasted for the trip here. I wonder if it will make it home in one piece."

They all laughed and drank to that too.

"Hey, you didn't record this wine in your cool new wine book."

Cassidy considered. It was an average Oregon Pinot, but she supposed she had to start somewhere. She slipped out the small book and the pen that Jo had given to her, and made quick notes. Holding the glass up to the light, she studied the tone: amber-gold rather than amber-pink. A quick nose revealed peach and pineapple. Again and she found honeydew melon. She rolled a taste around on her tongue, which rarely matched the nose, and noted down the mandarin orange and a hint of lemon and...sharp pepper?

Then she looked down at the plate of jalapeño crab hush puppies that had just been added to the table. Sharp pepper and a dill-rosemary dip.

"It's a crab theme tonight," Perrin announced, so her jabbing at an unknown menu had only appeared random.

Next came crab-and-avocado sushi and a platter crab nachos that could feed all three of them by itself.

Cassidy finished her entry and folded the book closed. She loved the feel of the dark, worked leather. Her first entry made it feel as if something important had happened, but she didn't know what. She was soon distracted by Perrin's happy chatter about the plans she had for her next dress designs for all three of them. It made time pass without seeming to touch them.

They were deep in their second round of drinks by the time Perrin finally wound down.

Cassidy shifted her focus to Jo who was looking a little blurred. She and Jo typically split a *glass* of wine when they were at one of Perrin's parties, not a *bottle*. She blinked hard a few times and still wasn't sure which of them was drifting out of focus.

"What are *you* celebrating?"

Jo brushed her hair back off her shoulders with an elegant sweep of her hand. It looked so smooth that Cassidy decided she was the one growing blurry.

"Well, you know that boutique law firm had called me to come back in."

She and Perrin leaned in closer to hear Jo's soft voice over a sudden round of noise in the bar.

"They really liked me and the questions I asked. I'm the only person they ever had who simply wanted an informational interview without expecting something from them. They offered me an internship for next summer. It doesn't pay anything, so I can't afford to take it, but—"

"You have to, Jo!" Perrin cut her off.

"By the end of second semester I'll have enough savings, so that I can afford to eat," Jo glanced down at the table, "not like this, but enough. What I can't afford is to live here in Seattle without a paying job."

Cassidy knew this was important to her roommate. She could read the pain of turning down the offer just in how perfectly still Jo sat. Cassidy knew there had to be an answer if she could just find it.

Squinting her eyes didn't help.

All it did was make the distant lights out the window flare.

The distant lights of—

She turned to Jo. "You're coming to live with me next summer. With me and Daddy. For free."

"No, Cassidy, I couldn't."

"Do you have somewhere better to go?" It was a low blow, Cassidy knew that Jo didn't, but it was too perfect an answer.

Jo looked down at the table and finally sighed deeply.

"Then it's settled. You'll call them tomorrow before we leave, and take the position."

She raised her wine glass, nearly empty for the second time and held it out toward Jo.

It took her a long moment, but she finally clinked her own against Cassidy's. Tears floated around the edges of her eyes, which she knew Jo hated to do.

So she turned to Perrin to clink glasses and give Jo a moment to recover.

For just a moment she spotted the haunted look on Perrin's face before she covered it with bravado and a glass clink.

*Next summer.* Cassidy knew that Perrin had nowhere to go, at least nowhere safe.

"You, too."

Perrin blinked at her in surprise. "Me too what?"

"You're going to be right here with us. Maybe you can intern with that lady who gave you the fabrics. Then you'd be just a block from Jo's office in Belltown." And maybe for herself she'd work at helping her dad's winery be more successful.

"Yeah, right. And maybe I'll just take over her store after college and become a world famous fashion designer." Perrin's voice was thick with sarcasm.

"Sure. You can do anything you want, Perrin. You have a real style."

Quiet Perrin returned and whispered so softly Cassidy had to lean close to hear, "Do you really think so?"

"I know so."

"And I can...come back...to..." Perrin looked as if she was even afraid to speak it. She glanced over her shoulder toward Bainbridge Island but didn't turn far enough to look.

"I promise."

"And your dad?"

"He'll love having the three of us in the house. He's so lonely that it will make up for me being gone so much."

"Are you sure?"

Cassidy nodded, "Positive." Though she and Daddy had never returned to the topic of Perrin as a friend.

Perrin grabbed her.

Cassidy was half afraid she was about to get kissed again, but instead Perrin just held her tightly. She could soon feel the tears running down both their cheeks where they were pressed together.

"Hey," Jo spoke up. "What just happened? Why are you both

crying? Rule Number Two, no crying unless we're all crying together."

Cassidy liked that rule and explained what had happened.

Quiet Perrin didn't say a word, but she didn't let go of Cassidy's hand for a long time. And sure enough, they were all soon crying together.

# CHAPTER 15

errin watched Vic Knowles as he hugged both Cassidy and Jo goodbye. She turned to make sure that she was busy loading the car when it would have been her turn.

She opened the trunk and—

"What's this?"

Cassidy's dad came up beside her. She tried to scoot aside but Cassidy and Jo had come up on her other side.

"It's a sewing machine."

The Singer machine had been folded into its wrought iron stand and the whole thing had been tucked in neatly along with her bag of fabric scraps.

"But it's your wife's." Perrin risked looking up at him. Except it wasn't up, it was down. He'd seemed so big and overwhelming in his house, but he was actually an inch shorter than she was.

"And it has sat collecting dust for most of Cassidy's life. My Adrianne wouldn't have liked that. She'd have wanted to see it used."

Perrin reached out and brushed a hand over the ironwork of the stand. She wanted it more than she wanted to breathe.

But the price. There was always a price.

"What do you want for it?" As if she didn't know.

He didn't hesitate. "Get good enough to make my daughter a beautiful dress and I'll be well paid."

For once in her life, Perrin didn't hesitate.

She simply wrapped her arms around him.

His arms came around her awkwardly, but finally patted her back a few times.

"I'll make her the most beautiful dress there's ever been," she whispered her promise.

He nodded, then released her. Just like that.

She took his hand in hers to keep him in place as the other two moved away to stow their own bags which would now have to squeeze into the backseat.

"Are you sure that you're okay with me being here this summer?" Perrin knew only too well that Vic Knowles thought her a bad influence. It had been obvious even before last night when they'd called him from the ferry landing. They'd all been too stumbling drunk to drive home despite standing out on the cold deck for the entire half-hour ferry ride.

"The wild girl does worry me, Perrin. *This* young woman? She is *always* welcome."

Perrin never blushed, nothing was past her limits—couldn't be with her past. But this time the heat rose to her cheeks until it burned there.

"I can't promise, Mr. Knowles. But I'll try. I promise that I'll really try."

This time she didn't shy away when he leaned in to peck her on the cheek. "That's good enough for me, Perrin."

# CHAPTER 16

*J*o sat in the back of the car, and wondered how her head could still be pounding from last night as they climbed over Snoqualmie Pass in the Washington Cascades, then continued east.

Perhaps it was the alcohol or perhaps the altitude.

Or maybe it was the phone call this morning. The partners had been elated at her change of mind. They'd even offered her a small stipend, enough to pay for some rent and food at Cassidy's.

Until now she hadn't considered environmental law but there was no question that it was going to be a huge growth sector in the 2000s and the decades to come. She knew of herself that she was always happier with a clear road map planned out.

She looked at her two friends chatting away in the front of the car. Cassidy who gave her heart so completely and Perrin who gave all her energy and passion. Both of those were areas that Jo knew she was woefully lacking. Yet when she was with them, she could pretend that she was more that way.

She stared out the side window as they crested the pass

between the high-banked snow berms that had been plowed aside, and began their long descent to the plains of eastern Washington. In forty hours they'd be back in college.

It was nice knowing they'd have the summer together, maybe even a couple summers. But how many people remained friends after college? She'd worked several events at school as part of her job in the alumni office. She'd seen the awkwardness of strangers who once thought they knew everything about each other and now couldn't remember each other's names without a surreptitious glance at their badges.

Was that what was going to happen to them?

No. She didn't want to lose them. These last days had been too important, too amazing. She'd never have come to Seattle without Cassidy's kindness, nor braved the law firms without knowing that Perrin wouldn't hesitate to go after what she wanted.

But how to stop it happening?

They were all the way to Minneapolis and she was once again in the back by the time she had an idea. Cassidy was driving, humming quietly to herself while Perrin slept in the passenger seat.

For the five hours to reach Chicago, she filled pages and pages on the pad in her leather portfolio but none of them were right.

She was barely aware of when the two of them switched and Cassidy asked if she wanted to move up front. Jo stayed in back despite the kind offer. Simple kindness was just what Cassidy did without even thinking about it.

Simple.

Maybe *that* was the answer. Jo flipped to a clean page and wrote quickly, then called out for Perrin to pull off at the next rest area.

There must have been more urgency in her voice than she intended, as Perrin pulled onto the shoulder in the midst of a

Chicago interchange like she was making a pit stop in a race car. They were against the rail on one side and maybe a foot from the roaring traffic on the other.

"What is it?" Perrin twisted around to look back at her. "You've been working on that for hours, it's gotta be awesome."

Cassidy pushed Perrin aside enough that she could turn to look back as well.

Jo tried to hand the pad forward but Cassidy shook her head. "Just read it aloud."

"It will sound…"

"Stupid?" Perrin laughed. "Hello, welcome to my life before I met you two."

"That's it. Well, both of it. Them."

Cassidy's smile steadied her.

"Yes, it will sound stupid, but also it's that I don't want to go back to before I met the two of you. I really don't want to lose either of you. Not now and not after college. So I drafted a contract."

Cassidy grinned, but Perrin was nodding fiercely as if it was a much smarter idea than it had sounded moments ago.

Trucks roared by, shaking their car as Jo began reading.

*"We the undersigned—"*

"I haven't signed anything yet," Perrin teased.

Cassidy shushed her.

*"—commit with all our hearts,"* she nodded toward Cassidy who blushed when Perrin knocked her knuckles on the top of Cassidy's head, *"that we will use all our energy and passion—"*

"That's me," Perrin chimed in.

*"—to ensure that we shall never lose touch with each other."*

The car became very quiet. Even the traffic roaring by outside seemed subdued.

"And then we need to sign it."

"No," Perrin was shaking her head in a confection-colored swirl.

Jo could feel herself collapsing. It had seemed so important and clear in her head just a moment ago. She must not have done it right. If she failed at this, would she fail this summer? And then at college? Would she fall all the way back to Ketchikan and end up slowly rotting on the bar stool next her father and the other regulars at the Crab Hole's bar?

"We need rules. I do *way* better with rules."

"She does," Cassidy acknowledged.

"Rules like what?"

"I dunno. Umm..." Perrin stared at the ceiling. "Like..."

Cassidy brightened, "Like Perrin's rule that our food doesn't have calories or fat if we're all drinking and eating together. That way, if we ever want to indulge guilt-free, we have to be together to do it."

"Rule Number One!" Perrin declared. "Yeah! Write that down. That's a good rule. And yours Jo, from last night. Or maybe it's two nights. Gods but we've been in this car forever. At Cutter's you said some rule."

"Rule Number Two," Jo spoke as she wrote, "we don't get to cry unless we're all crying together."

"That's it. Now Cassidy, it's your turn. Something that will make sure we have to be together. Come on. Make it like really amazingly amazing."

Cassidy stared at her helplessly, but Jo had no brilliant ideas.

Then her expression became thoughtful as she looked at Perrin. "I have an idea but I don't think it will work."

"Oh come on, you're the awesomest! Of course it will work. Tell us. Tell us." Perrin grabbed Cassidy's arm and physically shook her back and forth. "*Tell us!*"

Cassidy peeled off Perrin's hands but kept them in hers before speaking. "We're not allowed to get drunk, like out-of-control drunk—no, like judgement-impaired drunk, unless we're all together."

Jo had been truly drunk three times in her life including

their final night in Seattle, which she knew was one more than Cassidy.

Perrin looked everywhere except at the two of them. But neither did she let go of Cassidy's hands. She finally focused back on Cassidy.

"I don't know if I can do that." Her voice was barely louder than the muffled traffic.

"Perrin, you wowed every man in Cutter's with that dress you made in your third-ever week of sewing from a bag of scraps someone else threw out. You can do anything in the world you want to. I really and truly believe that."

"Me?"

"You."

Perrin twisted to look back at Jo, making the candy-stripes of her hair seem to twirl upward. "Do you think I can?"

Jo laughed. She couldn't help herself. Here she was doubting everything about herself, except her two friends. "Yes, absolutely anything."

"Okay," Perrin declared. "If Jo says I can, than it must be truth. We're like the three fates, only better—they're nothing but a bunch of cranky old biddies anyway. Truth," she pointed at Jo.

"Beauty," Cassidy pointed at Perrin.

"And heart," Perrin and Jo said in unison, making Cassidy blush again.

Jo wrote down the rule and all three of them solemnly signed it.

"We need a name," Cassidy said as she handed the pad back to Jo for safe keeping.

"Like the Three Fates?" Jo asked.

"Already taken. Besides, we're young and amazing; they're old and boring. Clotho the spinner, Lachesis the allotter controlling our lives, and Atropos the inflexible snipping them off."

"Ick," Cassidy agreed.

Jo looked down at their three names scribed below the three ridiculous rules and hoped that this would indeed work some form of magic and keep them together.

"I've got it!" Perrin declared gleefully. She then twisted back to drive and, with a hard gun of the engine, jumped them into the traffic using a tiny gap Jo never would have dared try.

"We're the Terrific Trio. Look out, world, here we come!"

# KEEP READING

Keep reading for an excerpt from book #1
of the small-town Oregon
Eagle Cove romance series:
*Return to Eagle Cove*
And reviews are a HUGE help.
Thanks for joining my journey, Matt.

IF YOU ENJOYED THIS, YOU MIGHT
ALSO ENJOY:

# RETURN TO EAGLE COVE (EXCERPT)

## A SMALL TOWN OREGON ROMANCE

"Almost home, sweetie."

"Oh joy," Jessica Baxter tried to clamp down on her sarcasm. It was a bad habit that worked fine in her social set back in Chicago, but sounded more petty with each mile they drove toward the Oregon Coast. She slumped down in the passenger seat of her mom's baby-blue Toyota hybrid. It still had that new car smell. As much as she'd dreamed of owning a hot sports car some day, she knew that she was enough her mother's daughter that this was probably the exact sort of eminently sensible car she would buy when her VW Beetle finally gave up the ghost.

Just like her mom.

Maybe she'd get it in red to be at least a *little* different.

Jessica sighed again, keeping it to herself so that she wasn't being overly offensive. Her mother was one of the many reasons that she'd gone as far away as possible for college and did her best to rarely return—she didn't want to turn into her mother and it was too easy to imagine doing so if she'd stayed in the small town of Eagle Cove, Oregon.

They were like twins separated by twenty-two years. The

two of them had been able to trade clothes since Jessica hit puberty and had shot up to match her mother's slender five-foot-ten. Other than a very brief mistake of dying her hair black as part of a tenth-grade dare, which had turned her fair complexion past goth and into bloodless vampire, they were both light blond.

The one part of twin-dom that she couldn't seem to pull off even though she wanted to was Mom's casual-chic. Monica Baxter was always dressed one step above the world around her; not fancy, just really well put together. The closest Jessica ever managed was Bohemian-chic which wasn't really the same thing, but she'd learned to make it her own. Of course, Bohemian was easier on the budget and often available in consignment stores which had only reinforced her chosen style.

Jessica did her best to not regress as they drove up into the Coast Range that separated the beach towns from the rest of Oregon...and failed miserably at that as well. She felt as if she was rapidly descending back toward being a pouty, pre-pubescent twelve from her present urban and worldly thirty-two.

Why did crossing the Oregon state line always take twenty years off her intelligence?

Maybe it was only Coast County. Because of the landscape the Oregon Coast felt incredibly far from anywhere. The Coast Range topped out at a mere four thousand feet high, but only a half dozen passes made it through the three hundred mile range of rugged hills that separated the beaches from the broad farming and industrial realm of the Willamette Valley. The interior of the state might as well be in a whole other country for how little it had in common with where she'd grown up.

"It's so strange being back here," Jessica rolled down the window and sniffed at the air. The scents were so rich and varied that they tickled. Bright with pine. Musty with undergrowth. Damp. A first hint of the sea.

"Well, it has been four years, honey. That's bound to make it seem a bit odd. But I'm so glad that you came."

"Me too, Mom." Better. She managed to say it as if she meant it, however unlikely that might be. Chicago fit her like a...but it didn't. The city was...something she was not going to give a single thought to for the next eight days. If she didn't fit there and she didn't want to fit in Eagle Cove, Oregon, then where did she belong?

Jessica breathed in deeply this time, trying to clear her thoughts with the fresh air of the Coast Range and nearly choked herself on how green everything smelled. The harsh slap of the mountains was almost an affront. The two-lane road dove and twisted along narrow corridors sliced through towering spruce and Douglas fir trees. The babies were sixty feet high along the shoulder as the car twisted up toward the pass; the mother trees behind them were much, much bigger.

And it wasn't just the trees that were lush. As they wound deeper into the Coast Range, each branch became covered with mosses and lichens. It soothed her eyes, so used to towering concrete and glass, with a living tapestry of greens, golds, and silvers. Beneath the trees grew an impenetrable tangle of salal and scrub alder. Old barns on the roadside didn't have shingle roofs, they had moss ones; some of them were covered inches thick. Many RVs, left unattended in front yards for too long, had a sheen of green growth on their north side.

"I really want to hate this," the Coast Range had three times the rainfall of Chicago, often surpassing a hundred inches a year. She expected to feel the weight of all that biomass crashing down on her shoulders, but instead she noticed the start of a disconcerting lightness as if coming home was a good thing. Jessica did *not* like that encroachment of pending appreciation, perhaps even enjoyment, upon her *true* feelings. "But it smells so good. Like sunshine and new growth."

Her mother's laugh was amused as they twisted along the two-lane road slowly climbing up a narrow valley.

"I didn't mean to say that out loud."

"But you said it anyway."

"Not helping, Mom."

Thankfully her mother's laugh said that she had understood Jessica's response as a tease. Which it mostly was, partly.

Jessica didn't *want* to like coming back to the coast. She didn't have small-town dreams. That was the main reason she'd left Eagle Cove. She had big city dreams…which weren't exactly coming together for her despite her efforts over the last fourteen years. But scurrying home wasn't going to fix those. And the selection of men in such a tiny town was, to put it kindly, pitiful. Puffin High—

Why they hadn't called it Eagle High in Eagle Cove was a subject of heated debate by every single class.

Puffin High's problem was that she knew every male her age all too well. The only reason the town had its own high school was that it was too far away from everywhere else for busing to make sense. Her senior class had just thirty-four students. Grades seven through twelve numbered under two hundred. And she knew far too much about every single one of them.

Even more obnoxiously invasive on her sense of right and wrong, instead of dumping rain, it was a perfect day. The sun sparkled down revealing a thousand shades of green in the living walls that lined the road. The air coming through the open window was thick with pine sap and the gentle tang of rotting undergrowth. There was so much oxygen in the air that it made her feel a little giddy.

Yes, a perfect day, if she'd been alone…and still in Chicago.

"I could have rented a car and saved you the drive, Mom." Actually, her budget had been thrilled when her mother had offered to come and fetch her. Also, once in Eagle Cove there wasn't a lot of use for a car, except when the rain poured down.

The whole town was only a few miles long and she could walk most places she'd want to go. As if there were any old haunts that she'd care to revisit. She'd made good her escape to Northwestern University's School of Journalism at eighteen but every now and then the town still sucked her back.

"Nonsense, honey. I'm always glad to drive up and get you. Besides, I needed a few things for the wedding."

"How many is this?" As if she didn't know. It took much of her journalistic skill to keep "that judgmental tone" out of her voice. Something her early teachers had dinged her on until she'd learned to eradicate it. But since she was regressing as they neared the coast, it was trying to make a comeback.

"Number four."

"Why, Mom?"

"Because I love the man." Her mother actually glanced away from the road to offer her a scowl. "I'd have thought that was obvious."

"It is. But you've divorced him three times."

"Because *your* father can drive a woman crazy without even trying." They giggled together because that was an absolute truth about Ralph Baxter.

"I meant, why marry him again? You're both legal age, your daughter lives in Chicago," and wouldn't complain if she lived on another planet entirely. "Just shack up together. Then you can lock the door whenever Daddy becomes too much like himself."

Ralph Baxter was always getting caught up in monster projects. Without a word of warning he would suddenly rip out the entire kitchen, once on the morning before a dinner party, because he'd thought of a better way to design it. Or he'd start building a new boat from scratch in the middle of the driveway, rather than in the generous side yard, which blocked parking near the house for months.

"Oh, honey. I'm too old fashioned a girl to 'just shack up.'"

Which was almost believable, even in the twenty-first century. To hear Aunt Gina—who despite her name was as not-Italian as a pastrami sandwich—tell it, Monica Lamont had chosen Ralph Baxter as her sweet sixteen love. She'd never even shopped around. How 1950s was that for a woman who hadn't even been born then?

Jessica had shopped plenty, or at least window-shopped. She'd found only a few men worth the cost of trying on for size. Definitely not a one worth taking home to keep. She might look like her mom, all blond, tall, and waiflike—which she kind of hated though the men seemed to like it—but inside she wanted to be like Aunt Gina.

Luigina Lamont looked nothing like her twin sister...or Grandpop...or much like Grandma for that matter. She was a statuesque redhead, in every voluptuous sense of the word and completely lived up to her name: Luigina meant "Famous Warrior." Her merry laugh slapped up against you at the most unexpected moments and constantly poked at your ticklish spot until you were curled up on the couch begging her to stop. Unlike Mom and her serial marriages to the same man, Gina brought home plenty yet had only tried to keep one.

That "unholy disaster" (as the family tales described it) had produced Natalya Daphne Lamont—Jessica's three-hour-older (and Natalya never let her forget it) first cousin and best friend. Just like Gina, Natalya didn't look like either her mom or Gina's brief husband. Maybe that was hereditary on that side of the family to balance out how much Jessica resembled her own mom and their shared grandma. Jessica had a sudden flash of her own future daughter looking just like her...and felt the world spin just a little at thinking about children at all.

"If I hadn't seen her come out between my legs myself," Aunt Gina would announce loudly, "I'd have thought I adopted the kid. Maybe I signed up to be a surrogate then forgot all about it."

Mom blushed every time Aunt Gina let that one loose in public, without understanding that if she didn't, Aunt Gina would have stopped long ago.

"Such an exotic offspring deserves an exotic name. Natalya for the Russian Bond girl in *GoldenEye* and Daphne for du Maurier the romance writer, *not* the nymph who had to turn into a tree to escape that lusty jerk Apollo." The fact that *GoldenEye* hadn't come out until Natalya had already been in grade school hadn't changed Aunt Gina's story one bit.

Maybe Jessica's own child would be lucky and take after Cousin Natalya who was slender like Jessica, but had all of the curves Jessica had prayed for throughout her teenage years but never been granted. Natya was also dusky skinned like a permanent tan and leggy like some French model. Jessica's and her mom's fairy light hair and Aunt Gina's mass of red curls had been transformed to a smooth cascade of dark chestnut on her cousin. Yet she and Jessica felt like twins from different mothers: one light, one dark, but much the same on the inside.

Jessica smiled at the sign as they cleared Maxine Pass: eight-hundred and three feet according to the sign. The "three" always made her laugh. It was like Becky, her other best friend from Eagle Cove, firmly insisting that she as five-four "and a quarter" as if it made a difference.

Maxine Pass was technically Maxwell Pass. Or it had been until the day that Aunt Gina had declared it just wasn't right for all of the passes to have male names merely because men were the ones who drew the maps back in the 1800s.

For her sixteenth birthday Jessica hadn't received her first kiss—already happened a year before—or gotten laid—two more years until that event. Instead, she'd been recruited for a "Mission!" At two in the morning on their shared birthday, Aunt Gina drove her and Natalya up to repaint the Maxwell Pass highway sign to Maxine. It had become a tradition that every time the highway department changed it back to Maxwell, the three of them would have a two a.m. gals' outing and change the sign once again. The highway department had given up years ago. A few of the more recent road maps had even changed the name.

"Girl Power!" they'd shout after each time they finished repainting the sign, usually about three a.m. Then they'd break out the thermos of hot chocolate and drink it from a shared cup while they admired their handiwork by moonlight.

One time Martin, the town cop, had shown up while they were doing it. Jessica and Natalya had ducked, but Gina hadn't slowed down a single brush stroke.

"Thought it would be you," Martin had observed through his open car window, obviously talking to Gina.

"Out of your jurisdiction, Marty," had been Aunt Gina's awesomely calm reply. She had always been Jessica's hero, but that totally clinched it. The town limits had been left far behind.

He'd joined them for the hot chocolate and had a good laugh at the "Girl Power!" chant.

Today Jessica just waved hello to the sign as they crested the pass and began their descent.

"Didn't you ever bust out, Mom?" Jessica tried to imagine her doing so, but couldn't quite conjure it up in her mind.

"Bust out? You mean cheat on your father? Never!"

"But what about between times, when you were divorced? That wouldn't be cheating."

Monica Lamont's lips thinned as she tightened her jaw and finally shook her head in a sharp little snap. "I was only living in the other end of the house."

"What about with Dad? You and Dad could just...you know?" The thought of her parents having sex was uncomfortable enough that she couldn't quite say it aloud.

"Ralph says that if I feel so strongly about things that I have to divorce him, then I shouldn't be expecting any special concessions while we are divorced."

Jessica felt she had to side with Dad on that one. He'd become used to his wife's antics, but that meant he didn't get any either in the interims. No wandering for him—it had always been clear that Ralph Baxter was absolutely crazy about Monica Lamont. Jessica felt kind of sorry for him.

"Wait. You mean you haven't had sex in two years?" This latest was their longest divorce yet.

Again that little snap that made Jessica's neck ache in sympathy. Mom moved to the right as the road added a climbing lane to reach the six-hundred and thirty-four foot (not quite so much bragging) Rogue Pass. That name at least made perfect sense by Oregon standards...because it wasn't anywhere near either of the two separate Rogue Rivers in Oregon. A half dozen cars roared past. Mom always drove exactly at the speed limit instead of the nearly mandatory ten over that prevailed throughout the state.

"So you're waiting for the wedding night?"

This time her mom's nod was a little sad.

"I'm sure tomorrow will be a great night, Mom."

At that she smiled brilliantly. "If the past three are anything to judge by, yes, it will be. It's just too bad we had to delay it."

"Delay it? Wait! What?" Jessica bolted upright in the car seat and almost throttled herself with her seatbelt. The wedding was supposed to be *tomorrow*. She'd secretly planned on staying just one day past the wedding, and then catching the Airporter Express that wandered through the small coastal towns once a day. She'd already warned Natalya to expect her in Portland for the rest of the week until her flight back to the Windy City.

"Well, we were meeting with Judge Slater about the ceremony. As he performed the first three weddings..."

Jessica resisted pointing out that he'd done all three divorces as well. Maybe her Oregon civility was coming back. Yeah, like a toothache.

"...and he had all of the old records in a file; even had the new marriage license pre-filled out, the dear man. However, it turns out that the first time we were married was on July fourteenth, not July seventh as I had remembered. You know how your father loves the cycle of things. So we moved the wedding to next weekend to coincide properly with the original. I knew you already had your plane tickets, so I didn't see any point in telling you."

Didn't see any point? She'd have moved heaven and earth to — Actually, her mother was right because she'd purchased the cheapest non-refundable, non-changeable tickets she could find.

A week! She was going to be trapped in Eagle Cove from Friday morning until Sunday morning nine days later? Oh, that was so bad.

"I can't believe that we celebrated it wrong for all of those years," her mother continued, completely oblivious to the panic she'd just created. "The seventh was the date that had always stuck in my head for our anniversaries."

Mom's dropping voice spoke volumes. She'd always been terrible at keeping a secret.

"So why *did* the seventh stick in your head?" Jessica kept it as casual as she could, rather than rubbing it in that her mom always gave up whatever she was trying to hide. It must be the journalist in her coming out: ask the question and then wait patiently for a reply. Not pushing was another change between them. Jessica didn't feel as if she was mellowing with age, but perhaps she was. Being disillusioned at thirty-two was no more newsworthy than it had been at twelve or twenty-two; but a woman shouldn't mellow until...well, maybe a hundred-and-two.

On the back side of Rogue Pass, Mom concentrated on the winding descent. Jessica waved at a massive Roosevelt elk who grazed in a small clearing beside the road. Coming back to

Eagle Cove might be only one step better than a nightmare, but it was a very scenic one. The road was soon joined by a stream rushing in a deep ravine on Jessica's side of the road; the problem was that they were both racing in the wrong direction —toward, not away from, her childhood home. The stream tumbled along almost as fast as they did down toward Eagle River which would eventually define the end of town where it opened into a broad bay before it reached the sea.

No one quite knew why the bay had been named a cove, but it showed that way on even the oldest maps. It gave the town an off-kilter personality to Jessica's mind, as if it was always seeking to find its true identity. No bridge crossed the Eagle to the wilderness area on the other bank. To reach that required either a boat or an hour drive back up to Highway 101, across the river, and then a long crawl back to the Coast over marginal logging roads.

"C'mon, Mom, give." Since not pushing at her mother had failed, Jessica went with regressing and shifted to the wheedling tone she'd perfected as a child. She might hate herself in the morning for slipping back into it, but it always worked. Sure enough, her mom gave in right on cue.

"July seventh was the one time we cheated. We didn't actually wait for our first wedding night," the blush on her mother's fair skin was almost bright enough to lighten the dark corridor between the towering trees. "Your father made it amazing. But that's also the day I became pregnant, though I didn't know it until after the wedding. All those years I was celebrating the wrong date. That's why we never fool around unless we're married."

"Sounds like you were celebrating *exactly* the right date, Mom." She tried to pin down the exact date of her own first time, but it hadn't been all that memorable. Good, but "earth-shattering" was just another one of those 1950s' myths that didn't happen in the twenty-first century. Except, apparently, for her own mother. How unfair was that.

"Maybe," her mom admitted, "but we're going to get married on the fourteenth anyway."

"So, I'm illegitimate?" Not that it bothered her, but she couldn't resist needling her mother about it. Maybe she hadn't matured all that much.

"Yes dear, but only by one week. I swear I didn't know." This time Jessica heard that her mom's confession was a sigh at Jessica's question rather than sounding contrite. Maybe it was time Jessica grew up a bit—even when in Eagle Cove.

"Does Aunt Gina know about all this?"

"No one does, except your father and now you. You only arrived three days early, which was actually four days late. No one gave it any thought."

*Excellent!* Forget being mature. Aunt Gina would love the extra dirt for teasing her sister and Jessica couldn't wait to be the one to tickle her aunt's funny bone.

# # #

It had been another long morning of assisting the Judge— always with a capital J. Monday through Friday, six a.m. to ten, Greg Slater helped his father. At first it had been something that Greg did to help out, but he'd come to like the simple routines and structure to his mornings.

"Ready?" he called back to the kitchen as he did every day. There was no real need to ask. The big old clock hung high on the wall said it was exactly six a.m. and the Judge was a very punctual man.

But Greg looked for the solemn nod before moving out into the diner and flicking on the fluorescents, "The Puffin Diner" sign, and the porch lights. There wasn't much need for the last, sunrise was twenty minutes ago, but the sun itself wouldn't clear the Coast Range ridge until at least six-thirty. For now,

Beach Way, the town's main street, was mostly cool shadows and darkened buildings.

The bell mounted on the back of the door rang almost right away as Cal Mason Jr. came in. Greg had already set a mug of coffee on the counter for him. Cal ran the Blackbird Bakery and was hours into his day. Five days a week he was as punctual as the Judge. Cal Sr. wouldn't be in for a few hours yet.

"Your standard, Cal?"

"Double," though Greg knew that was a joke. Cal was one of the few men in town big enough that he could have eaten two of the Judge's generous portions. Six-two and as powerful as a bulldozer; his hands dwarfed the coffee mug.

Because Cal sat at the six-stool wooden counter, the Judge was less than five feet away through the broad service window that connected the dining room with the kitchen, but he waited for Greg to fill out the order slip and clip it to the spinner.

It was Greg's own fault. The diner's service had been a bone of contention, or rather "lengthy negotiation" just as most things were with the Judge.

"They can pick up their own plates at the window. Coffee pot is right there behind the counter where anyone who wants a refill can get their own."

Greg had won that round by subterfuge. He'd numbered the tables and then only put the numbers on the order slips, making it impossible for the Judge to boom out with "Veronica, your order is up." Customers had slowly adapted to not having to leave their tables for every little thing.

At least Greg thought he'd won, until a full three weeks later his father had winked at him while sliding across a short stack with bacon and hash browns for Karen Thompson, "Like I don't know who orders what on a Thursday."

Now the Judge wouldn't cook a thing without a proper ticket. Well, he'd cook it, but he wouldn't serve it no matter how busy or harried Greg was.

Cal's plate came up less than thirty seconds after Greg hung the ticket just as it did every morning: western omelet, hash browns, farm sausage, and English muffin. The last was about the only kind of bread that Cal didn't bake.

"Gotta have something that I can order out for and enjoy without baking it myself."

Greg moved the plate across to the counter and refilled Cal's half-drained mug of coffee.

There wasn't much call for a judge in a town the size of Eagle Cove. Semi-retired for the last five years, he no longer spent three days a week in Newport to sit on the bench as he had throughout Greg's childhood. Instead he'd set up a small courtroom in town. He mainly handled family matters like marriages and estates, and fines for drunk and disorderly tourists who soon learned that Judge Slater was a fierce protector of the town. There was only the occasional speeding ticket—no matter how hard Martin the cop tried to catch someone. The town was perched against the Pacific Ocean at the dead end of a winding two-lane that had left the coastal highway a dozen miles back; it had enough "Sharp Curves Ahead" signs to quell even the most lead-footed of souls.

So, "for something to keep me busy," the Judge held office hours only in the afternoons because his weekday mornings were all spent working as a short-order cook. And ever since Greg's return to Eagle Cove three years ago, he'd been his father's front-of-house man: waiter, cashier, and busboy.

The Puffin Diner had been a near derelict before his dad had bought and reopened it. It was a classic small town place built to serve the early morning fishermen, especially those returning from a long night's work on the offshore shoals; it was little changed over the last ninety years.

The clapboard building stood high enough on a heavy stone foundation that even the Christmas storm flood of 1964 had crested two steps below the front entry. It was one of the only structures on the town's main street that didn't have a street-level entry. All of the other businesses that had existed then had high-water lines drawn halfway or more up their walls. The Grouse Hardware store, the lowest spot in town close beside the docks, had a small wooden plaque of a fish screwed in just above the main door lintel. It was bright yellow with "Dec 22, 1964" painted on it in tropical blue—it was generally considered to be a little boastful, but old man Jaspar refused to tone down the color scheme that he'd painted on that fish in his youth.

The interior of the diner was so retro that it would have been ironic-modern if it wasn't quite so authentic. The steel-edged tables of blue Formica were scuffed nearly colorless by the thousands of plates and silverware settings that had been slid across their surfaces over the years. The chairs' red leather was sun-faded and the old chrome had pitted with rust from the salt air, making them uncomfortable to the touch without quite being painful. The linoleum floor had been replaced...back in the 1980s when mauve and hunter green had been trendy colors. The six round stools bolted to the floor at the counter squealed every time someone spun on or off them. The kitchen was authentic right down to the large service window, the steel spinner rack for order slips dangling in one corner, and the big grill and burners in the back. The scents of eggs, hash browns, and frying bacon filled the main street each morning enticing all passersby to come and find comfort food.

Ralph Baxter and Manny McCall came in and took their usual spot by the corner window. They'd have tourists out fishing off their boats within the hour and were both after black coffee and tall stacks.

At first Greg had resented serving the Judge's fare—it was as invariable as his father. Scrambles, omelets, pancakes—no waffles because the iron had broken the same day Mom had died and he couldn't seem to fix it and wouldn't let Greg try.

The pancakes were big and fluffy. The very crispy hash browns were not an option; they were on every single plate, even with the pancakes. Farm fresh sausage or bacon was the other staple on every plate—not that it was a choice. Everyone received whichever Carl Parker had delivered the day before along with the eggs.

All of Greg's efforts to vary the oatmeal recipe, served with bacon or sausage and hash browns of course, had been in vain. The Judge served only rolled oats—not steel cut—with sliced, not diced, dried apricots and diced, not sliced, fresh apple. Whether brown sugar or maple syrup was used to sweeten it was wholly up to the customer; local honey was also available.

Omelets were the Judge's real specialty and by six-thirty there were already a dozen slips up for them. Omelets were the only dish where variations were allowed. He offered them with cheese, mushrooms, or smoked salmon fillings. Never all three of course, because there were limits to what was proper.

The Puffin Diner mostly served coffee. Greg's sole triumph at adjusting the menu had been when he managed to switch from Dad's "fresh ground" granules purchased in large plastic tubs to fresh-ground French roast. Tea or hot chocolate were the only other options, but asking for marshmallows with the latter was frowned upon unless you were a kid—the whipped cream came out of a spray can.

They'd fought royally over the Judge's inflexibility, but of course fighting over things was a tradition in the Slater household. Not that voices were ever raised, because that would never do. The few times Greg had tried that tactic he'd been ruled "Out of Order" and banished from the dinner table: the sole forum for Slater "discussions." With Ma gone to cancer three years before—Greg's original reason for returning to Eagle Cove—he didn't have the heart to "force" the Judge into driving him from the table after that first time. When he'd been remanded to the kitchen two weeks after Mom's funeral, he'd made the mistake of glancing back as he'd moved off to finish his meal. His father had looked old, sad, and impossibly alone.

Greg hadn't been able to face living in the big old house out on the beach, so he'd moved into the guest house. Once he finally understood that no number of cogent debates were going to sway the Judge, Greg had let the menu go. It had been unchanged in either content or price in the last decade—other than the wavy black line of magic marker through the "Waffles (with blueberries when in season)."

Greg had been on the verge of leaving town when the Judge sat him down at the big house's dining room table. Ma Slater had been in the ground for a month. Greg knew he didn't really have anywhere to go, he'd learned all he was going to from the banquet chef at the Sorrento Hotel in Seattle and there weren't any top positions open for an untested executive chef wanting to make his mark. He didn't have the capital to make his own splash, not in the insanely competitive restaurant markets in the big cities. But he'd find something.

"Been watching you, son. Been tasting your food," the Judge had tapped a fork on his dinner plate. Greg had roasted a pair of fresh-caught trout in hazelnut butter with a dressing of spring greens and homemade basil vinegar. Though Greg had cooked half the meals since Ma's funeral—"fair is fair" the Judge had declared—it was the first time his father had spoken of it.

"Uh-huh," Greg had gone for a neutral acknowledgement. He knew the Judge hated such prevarications, but Greg didn't know where this was heading and went for caution.

"This is good. Real good."

Greg hadn't been able to offer even a neutral grunt over his surprise at the Judge's remark.

"Still needs some work, though."

Before Greg could snap at him about what did a man who scrambled eggs and ruled on law know about fine cuisine, the Judge continued.

"You need more seasoning," and he aimed a fork at Greg's chest, "and I'm not talking about salt. Your technique is the best I've ever seen, but I don't taste anything special. There's nothing here that isn't in any other fine restaurant. You need time to find your own voice, not some other chef's."

"My own voice?" But he didn't need to ask, he'd heard it a thousand times growing up.

The Judge looked down at the trout, one of the only times he'd ever said anything without looking at whoever he was addressing straight in the eye, "Your mother taught me that."

Ma had been a painter, a good one. Her seascapes had sold in galleries up and down the coast. Tillamook, Newport, Gold Beach, they all snapped up as much as she could produce and was willing to let go of—Grosbeak Gallery in town had always gotten first pick though. She'd often talked about finding your voice in your art so that it didn't look like everyone else's.

"So, here is the deal I'm offering you."

Greg knew that it wouldn't be open to negotiation; no one negotiated one of Judge Slater's "deals."

"The diner is mine on weekdays from six to ten every morning. I'd like you to stay as my assistant because you're good at it. That pays rent here at the house, a small salary, and we split the tips. What you do with the diner for the rest of the time, that's up to you."

And for three years, Greg had stayed in Eagle Cove and searched for his own voice. In the first year, he'd never cooked for anyone but himself and his father—who never again spoke about the food itself. Then one night Greg had invited a couple of buddies from high school who were still in town to the diner, as a test audience. Word got out about how good it was and folks had started asking when he'd do it again.

He'd eventually started "Irregular Friday Dinners at The Puffin." He only opened when he had a new meal to test. It was all *prix fixe,* fixed price—a twenty in the jar—and a set menu.

After two years of those he felt almost ready to take his cooking out into the world; maybe spend a while as a pop-up restaurant —there and gone—rather than a full launch. He'd been saving his half of every morning tip and every cent for when he went back to the cities. At first he'd simply been trying to be better by the time he left Eagle Cove, but he'd become obsessed with finding and perfecting his "chef's voice." He wanted it to be so clear that it was undeniable. When he went back to Seattle, no one would label him the protégé of Charlene at Maximilien's or Angelo at The Tuscan Hearth. He'd be his own—

The old brass bell screwed into the top of the diner's front door rang like a small ship was coming into port. Morning service peaked as usual around eight and had now tapered off to just a few lingering diners.

Greg glanced at the big-face clock above the cash register— 9:57—and suppressed a groan. Judge's rule was that if you were in the door by ten, you could take as long as you wanted. If it was ten sharp plus a second, you were turned away—"Fair is fair." Maybe they'd be quick; he'd had an idea for a savory roulade that he wanted to try out.

Greg turned back and had to blink, then blink again. The morning sunlight shone through the front window and silhouetted two dazzling blondes, their hair practically set afire by the sunlight streaming in from behind them.

Then his eyes adapted as they moved farther into the room.

Mrs. Baxter who was soon to be Mrs. Baxter once again.

And a woman he hadn't seen since the day she'd left for college, but he'd know anywhere.

Jessica matched his own five-ten and her hair, instead of being the waist-long waterfall he'd remembered, now floated about her shoulders in choppy wisps that framed a face of high cheekbones, full lips, and eyes that sparkled with mischief.

Halfway across the old linoleum floor, she stopped and looked at him.

"Greggie's gaping, Mom."
And he couldn't do a thing about it.

---

Keep reading.
Available at fine retailers everywhere:
*Return to Eagle Cove*

# ABOUT THE AUTHOR

USA Today and Amazon #1 Bestseller M. L. "Matt" Buchman has 70+ contemporary and military romance novels, and action-adventure thrillers. Also 100 short stories and lotsa audiobooks.

Booklist says: 3x "Top 10 Romance of the Year" and among "The 20 Best Romantic Suspense Novels: Modern Master-pieces." NPR and B&N say: "Best 5 Romance of the Year." PW declares: "Tom Clancy fans open to a strong female lead will clamor for more."

A project manager with a geophysics degree, he's designed and built houses, flown and jumped out of planes, solo-sailed a 50' sailboat, and bicycled solo around the world…and he quilts. More at: www.mlbuchman.com.

# Other works by M. L. Buchman: *(\* - also in audio)*

## Action-Adventure Thrillers

### Dead Chef
One Chef!
Two Chef!

### Miranda Chase
Drone*
Thunderbolt*
Condor*
Ghostrider*
Raider*
Chinook*
Havoc*
White Top*

## Romantic Suspense

### Delta Force
Target Engaged*
Heart Strike*
Wild Justice*
Midnight Trust*

### Firehawks
**MAIN FLIGHT**
Pure Heat
Full Blaze
Hot Point*
Flash of Fire*
Wild Fire

**SMOKEJUMPERS**
Wildfire at Dawn*
Wildfire at Larch Creek*
Wildfire on the Skagit*

### The Night Stalkers
**MAIN FLIGHT**
The Night Is Mine
I Own the Dawn
Wait Until Dark
Take Over at Midnight

Light Up the Night
Bring On the Dusk
By Break of Day
**AND THE NAVY**
Christmas at Steel Beach
Christmas at Peleliu Cove
**WHITE HOUSE HOLIDAY**
Daniel's Christmas*
Frank's Independence Day*
Peter's Christmas*
Zachary's Christmas*
Roy's Independence Day*
Damien's Christmas*
**5E**
Target of the Heart
Target Lock on Love
Target of Mine
Target of One's Own

### Shadow Force: Psi
At the Slightest Sound*
At the Quietest Word*
At the Merest Glance*
At the Clearest Sensation*

### White House Protection Force
Off the Leash*
On Your Mark*
In the Weeds*

## Contemporary Romance

### Eagle Cove
Return to Eagle Cove
Recipe for Eagle Cove
Longing for Eagle Cove
Keepsake for Eagle Cove

### Henderson's Ranch
Nathan's Big Sky*
Big Sky, Loyal Heart*
Big Sky Dog Whisperer*

# Other works by M. L. Buchman:

## Contemporary Romance (cont)

### Love Abroad
*Heart of the Cotswolds: England*
*Path of Love: Cinque Terre, Italy*

### Where Dreams
*Where Dreams are Born*
*Where Dreams Reside*
*Where Dreams Are of Christmas\**
*Where Dreams Unfold*
*Where Dreams Are Written*
*Where Dreams Continue*

## Science Fiction / Fantasy

### Deities Anonymous
*Cookbook from Hell: Reheated*
*Saviors 101*

### Single Titles
*The Nara Reaction*
*Monk's Maze*
*the Me and Elsie Chronicles*

## Non-Fiction

### Strategies for Success
*Managing Your Inner Artist/Writer*
*Estate Planning for Authors\**
*Character Voice*
*Narrate and Record Your Own Audiobook\**

# Short Story Series by M. L. Buchman:

## Romantic Suspense

### Antarctic Ice Fliers

### Delta Force
*Th Delta Force Shooters*
*The Delta Force Warriors*

### Firehawks
*The Firehawks Lookouts*
*The Firehawks Hotshots*
*The Firebirds*

### The Night Stalkers
*The Night Stalkers 5D Stories*
*The Night Stalkers 5E Stories*
*The Night Stalkers CSAR*
*The Night Stalkers Wedding Stories*

### US Coast Guard

### White House Protection Force

## Contemporary Romance

### Eagle Cove

### Henderson's Ranch\*

### Where Dreams

## Action-Adventure Thrillers

### Dead Chef

### Miranda Chase Origin Stories

## Science Fiction / Fantasy

### Deities Anonymous

### Other
*The Future Night Stalkers*
*Single Titles*

# SIGN UP FOR M. L. BUCHMAN'S NEWSLETTER TODAY

*and receive:*
*Release News*
*Free Short Stories*
*a Free Starter Collection*

*Do it today. Do it now.*
*www.mlbuchman.com/newsletter*